postcards from PISMO

DISCARD

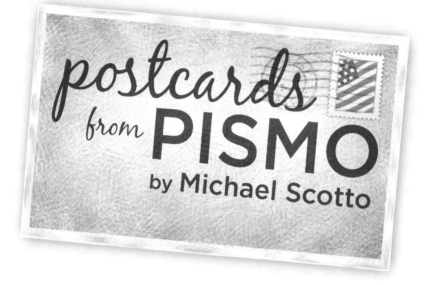

A novel by Michael Scotto

Illustrations by Dion Williams

Midlandia Press

Beaver, Pennsylvania

© National Network of Digital Schools 2012

Midlandia Press
An imprint of NNDS Corporation
1000 Third Street
Beaver, PA 15009
All rights reserved.

Visit us on the web at
http://www.midlandiapress.com.

Midlandia® is a registered trademark of National Network of Digital Schools Management Foundation.

Edited by Ashley Mortimer
Typography by Kent Kerr
Mr. Cesar illustration by Kent Kerr

ISBN-13: 978-0-9837243-6-0 (ISBN-10: 0983724369)

Library of Congress Control Number: 2011943050

2 4 6 8 10 9 7 5 3 1

Printed in the USA.

First printing, May 2012.

To all who serve, at home and abroad

Dear Soldier,

I'll bet you weren't expecting a letter from me, were you? It would be pretty weird if you were, us being total strangers and all. I don't know you, and you don't know me. Since I am the one writing the letter, I'll start.

Hi! My name is Felix Maldonado. I am in fourth grade. I come from a town called Pismo Beach, California. Maybe you have heard of it. It is in the Central Coast part of California. The city nearby is San Luis Obispo.

I live with my dad, my mom, and my brother, Quin. Dad owns a shop near our house. He rents ATVs for people to ride on the beach. (That's short for "all-terrain vehicles," in case you didn't know.) Mom is a photographer. Quin is a senior in high school, but he graduates next month. I don't know what he'll be next.

This week, everyone in my class is writing to a soldier. I hope this letter gets to you in time for Memorial Day. Mrs. Seymour says that it takes two weeks for a letter to get all the way to Afghanistan. (She also wrote how to spell that on the board.) I asked why we don't just send emails instead, since they're a lot faster. She said that wasn't the point.

Either way, I am writing this letter to say thank you. Thank you for being so brave, and thank you for leaving your family to fight for our country. I don't think I could do something like that. I couldn't even go away to camp in Big Sur last summer, and that was only one hundred miles away. It's not even out of the state! I guess I'm just not very brave.

I'm not sure what else to say about myself. My favorite animal is a horse. I like reading comic books. I also like movies about sports, even though I am not good at sports. Do you ever get to watch movies in Afghanistan?

I know you are in a very dangerous place. And you're very busy, too. Mrs. Seymour told us that you won't have time to write back. But I hope you prove her wrong. To save you some time, I have a list of questions you could answer, besides the movie question. Here they are:

1. What is your name and where are you from?
2. How long have you been in the Army?
3. What do soldiers really do?
4. Is it true that you guys use a lot of swear words?
5. Do you ever get scared?

You do not have to write me back if you are too busy. This was my class project, not yours. But I would like it if you did. It would be cool to make a new friend. The return address on the envelope is for my school. School lets out next month, so if you do want to write, write back soon!

Please be safe,
Felix Maldonado, Room 17B

P.S. If soldiers really do swear a lot,
please do not swear if you write me
back. I don't think Mrs. Seymour will let
me read your letter if you do.

June 13th

Dear Lt. Greene,

You wrote me back! I can't believe it. I was hoping that you would. I don't know if you noticed, but I put a lot of work into my letter. Actually, I think I got a little carried away. The other kids' letters were one page, and mine was a whole two pages without even writing double-spaced. I'm pretty sure it was the longest thing I've ever written. Seriously! I don't know how people lived before computers. There were a lot of folks walking around with sore hands from having to write everything, I'll bet.

It was really cool to get your letter. I've never gotten a letter from another country before, except for the Philippines. That's where my ancestors are from. I still have cousins there who send us a card every Christmas. But now I have gotten mail from America, the Philippines, _and_ Afghanistan. Mrs. Seymour had me read the whole thing in front of the class! That sure made Roger Batista give me the evil eye. I think it made some of the other kids jealous, too. That's because you are the only soldier who wrote back!

And you were just in time, too. School gets out on Friday. If any more soldiers write back after then, the kids won't get the letters. They'll probably just be lost. I wonder what my school does with all of the mail that comes over the summer. Where do all the bills go?

I'm getting off track, though. That's a problem I have sometimes. I feel like I have too many thoughts banging around in my head. Before I can get some of the old thoughts out, I have new ones that get in the way.

It doesn't really matter about the school mail anyway, at least not for us. Now that we are friends, you can have the address to my dad's ATV shop. That's the return address on the envelope. I'll probably be helping Dad out this summer, so just write me there.

Thanks for answering my questions—and for not swearing while you did it! (Ha-ha.) And thanks for asking me some questions back. It'll really help me to be a better pen pal.

But before I get into that, I have to say that you are younger than I thought you would be! You're only a few years older than Quin, and he's just in high school. (For a few more days, anyway.) It's awesome that you are a Lieutenant 1st Class even though you've only been in the Army for a year. That's a pretty high rank, isn't it? You must be really good at your job to move up so fast.

Well, I was all set to tell you more about Pismo Beach and my family like you asked, but my hand is getting tired again. You can probably tell from my handwriting.

Your pen pal,
Felix
Student 3rd Class (kidding)

P.S. When I read your letter to the class, I didn't actually read the whole thing. I skipped over the part about how you get scared sometimes on your patrols. I wasn't sure if you'd want everybody to know. But thanks for being honest with me. It makes me feel better to know that even soldiers get scared. I'm scared of a lot of things.

Dear Sir,

Sorry I ran out of steam last night. I was really planning on answering all of your questions. On the plus side, now you get two letters instead of only one!

A new letter also gives me a chance to try out a new greeting. Which one do you like better: Sir or Lt. Greene? Or do you want 1st Lt. Marcus Greene, US Army? You can sign your letters however you want, but that is an awful lot to write every time I want to say hi.

I was reading your letter again. You know, I had no idea that Army men did so many different kinds of things! I kind of thought you guys just did fighting. Pretty silly, right?

It made me think of more questions, though. Like, when you bring medicine to a village, what kinds of medicine do you bring? Do you bring inhalers? I'm wondering because I use an inhaler sometimes. I want to know if kids in Afghanistan get asthma, too.

But I should start answering your questions before I ask any more of my own. It's only fair. So…here we go!

1.   <u>What do you look like?</u>

I look like a million dollars!

Actually, I am mostly average looking. I would send you a photo, but my class picture from this year is just lousy. I had an alfalfa sprout sticking up on the back of my head and the photographer didn't say a word about it! So, I will just tell you that I have straight black hair and tan skin. That's partly because the sun is really strong here, but it's also part of my Filipino good looks. (That's what my dad says.)

Do any Filipinos live in Kansas? I'll be honest…I don't know much about it except that:

1. It is flat.
2. It is sort of boxy-shaped.
3. There is a lot of corn.
4. You are from there.

When I was a baby, I got the nickname Peanut because I was so small. I'm normal height now, but still not normal weight. I'm really skinny, the skinniest kid in my class. I can eat whatever I want and it never seems to stick. I hate it. But whenever I complain about it, my mom will just pat my dad on the belly and say, "Enjoy it while it lasts!"

But how am I supposed to do that? Nobody thinks it's cool that I'm so skinny. It's not like I'm the Amazing Felix to them, with super stomach powers. Kids already give me trouble because most of my clothes come from the thrift shop and my mom makes me carry around my brother's old cell phone, which is so old it doesn't even have a camera in it! I wish I wasn't skin-and-bones on top of it. I know everybody says you shouldn't care what other people think of you, but it's really hard to ignore how they act.

Take Roger Batista from class. His family owns a nice little hotel over near the cliffs. You'd think people with such a nice hotel would raise a nice kid. But they didn't. Roger is rotten. Just last week, he and his friends Lupe and Kenneth spent all recess running right into me and knocking me over. Each time I got mad, they'd pretend it was an accident, like, "Oh, sorry, I didn't even see you there. You must've turned sideways." I can't wait for school to end on Friday, I really can't.

Sorry I'm complaining so much. My problems probably seem pretty dumb to someone fighting in a war. I guess those kids just bother me more than I let on most times. If you have any special advice about bullies, I'd love to have it.

Anyway, Mom just called me for dinner and Dad doesn't like to wait to eat after he gets home from the shop. We're having burgers, and Mom made cassava cake for after. (That's a dessert from the Philippines. I wish I could mail you some.)

I just had an idea! Maybe tonight I'll eat two burgers instead of one, and I'll have a huge piece of sticky cassava cake with a mountain of whipped cream for dessert. Then I'll wash it down with cold milk, and the whole time I'll wiggle my butt and go, "Mm-mm-mm! I sure do enjoy being skinny!"

Yikes. That's a silly idea. I guess this is why I should write in pencil and not pen, like Mrs. Seymour always says.

Thanks for reading,
Felix the Nut

Dear Lt. Greene,

I told my family about how we are pen pals. Mom thinks it is nice that I am keeping you company since you don't have any family of your own. Is it hard not to have a family? Sorry if that is rude or a dumb question. I just can't even imagine what it would be like.

Anyway, Mom is also proud that I am being kind and writing and using my creativity. She even took a picture of me that I could send to you! She's a lot better at taking pictures than our dopey school photographer.

Quin wants me to ask you more questions about being a soldier. I told him, "Get your own pen pal!"

Dad said that he hopes I am not going to be a bother to you. But I can tell that he is proud, too, because of how he said it. He peeked his nose up over the newspaper he was reading and said it like, "Just don't be a pest, Peanut." I could hear the smile on his face, if that makes sense.

Anyway, my family likes that you are my friend and that I am your friend. There's really only one problem with this whole deal: writing letters takes <u>FOREVER</u>! It takes a long time to write down everything I am thinking. Plus, there is no spell-check except for my brain, so I have to write extra carefully. And as if that didn't take enough time, then I have to mail it. It'll be weeks before you get this note, and weeks more 'til I get your letter back. My whole life could change and you'd be way behind.

So I was wondering...do you have email in Afghanistan? I don't have an email address of my own, just the one that my parents use. But I bet I could get one if I asked. Other kids in my class have their own email addresses, and it would mostly be for us anyway. It would just be much faster to be email buddies instead of pen pals.

If you don't have email, I won't be mad. Maybe forget I said anything. I'd like writing to you on paper or over the Internet.

Either way, I'll keep writing letters until I hear back. But I have to rest my arm now. I'll start back on your questions tomorrow, I promise.

Take care,
Felix

ENCLOSURE: Photo of me! (This is how they did attachments in the olden days.)

Dear Lt. Greene,

This is Felix Maldonado, reporting to you live from sunny Pismo Beach!

I'm just funning around. All your questions just made me think of giving a report, which made me think of the guys on the news. Anyway, here's your next question.

2. <u>What is your town like?</u>

All kinds of people visit Pismo every year. That's how most of the families who live here make their money, from the tourists. It's sunny here a lot, and it never gets too hot or cold. During the day you never need to wear much more than a hoodie. A lot of shops sell them, with "Pismo Beach" printed right on the front. But only the tourists wear those ones.

The water gets too cold to splash in sometimes, but it's okay to surf if you have a wetsuit to keep warm. A lot of kids from Cal Poly come here to surf. That's the big college over in San Luis Obispo. It's a good school. Quin wanted to go next fall, but it "just wasn't in the cards," to quote my dad. (That's Dad's way of saying that we couldn't afford to pay for it.)

People also come here to dig for clams. Pismo clams are much bigger than the clams on the rest of the coast. You have to get a license to go clamming, but that's pretty easy. You can get one at the drugstore. We have a Clam Festival every October with a parade and everything.

Our beach is famous for other non-clam reasons, too. It's been in photo shoots for magazines, and movie people come film in the dunes a few miles away. If they want to film an ocean scene, they point the cameras one way. If they want to film a desert scene, they turn the cameras the other way and pretend the ocean isn't there. Can you believe that?

It's not like folks from Hollywood are here all the time, though. Mostly it's regular people. They come and camp on the beach. They set up tents right in the sand, near the shore or in the dunes. They can go for a drive in the sand if they want. You can drive your own car right on the beach, but you'll get around better in something with big, fat tires. That's why my dad rents ATVs.

Mom sells some of her photographs at our shop, too. She turns the pictures into postcards with our computer and sells them that way. She is really talented. Between the both of them, we make enough to get by. "Just enough," Dad says when he and Mom write up the monthly budget.

We're not poor, I don't think. But I still have to share a bedroom with

Quin. We have one bedroom for the parents, one bedroom for the kids…and one bathroom for the "all of us." We live on a street called Ocean View, except that's sort of a trick name. I'll tell you why.

You can view the ocean on Ocean View…except not on the part of it where we live. On our block, you can view big mountains in one direction and Highway 101 in the other. There's a railroad track nearby, but the trees across the street block my view of that, too. The best I get is that I can hear the trains pass sometimes.

It used to make me mad that we have basically the worst block in all of Pismo Beach. But now that I'm ten, I'm allowed to ride my bike around a lot more in the daytime. I can't ride fast or up steep hills, but I can go far. For example, I'm allowed to ride the whole three miles to Dad's shop. I just have to bring my inhaler and my clunky old cell phone.

Sometimes I ride to the pier and watch the tourists. On clear days the pier gets packed. But you know what a lot of tourists do rather than enjoy the view? They do weird things like take pictures of the seagulls there, as if they're some kind of rare bird. Some tourists use the pier to fish, too, but I wouldn't eat pier fish. The gulls do their business right in the water there. Sick!

The pier is really popular, and so is the Promenade, which is like a shopping and fun area that's next to the pier. But I know a better spot to look at the ocean. I found it a few months ago. That's the cliffs, the ones near the Batista family's hotel. It's really scary near the edge of the cliffs, especially if there is fog, but if I stay near the hotel's fence, it's great. When I feel bad, I like to go sit on the rocks there and touch the moss with my hands and think. The rocks and the water and the waves are so big that they make my worries feel small.

Tune in next time,
Felix

P.S. I'm trying to think of a movie that shows our beach, but I can't think of one right now. I'll ask my mom about it later.

Dear Lt. Greene,

Yes! Today I officially graduated from the fourth grade!!! Goodbye, homework...hello, summer!

I guess I was saying all of that out loud just now as I wrote it down, because Quin is laughing at me. He's in our room. He finished high school today, and now he's getting dressed up to go to a party with his friends.

Quin's still laughing. I guess I mumbled all of that, too. I kind of do that whenever I write. I like to write alone when I can.

Here are the things I am saying back to him:

"Bug off, Quin!"
"Quit it!"
"A girl's never going to talk to you if you wear that shirt."

That last one kind of shut him up, ha-ha.

Okay, Quin's out for the night. Dad's not here, either. He's at the shop still, doing repairs on a Kawasaki that broke down. That's a kind of ATV. Some dummy burnt the clutch, so Dad is putting in a new one before tomorrow.

So it's just me and Mom, and she promised we could have a movie night tonight. She said she's proud of Quin, but she's proud of me, too. I can pick any two movies we have as long as they're less than two hours each. I'm glad the next couple of questions you asked are easy ones.

3. <u>What is your favorite subject in school?</u>

None! I am out of school, ha-ha!

But if you meant what <u>was</u> my favorite subject, this year it was probably science. Mrs. Seymour had us do neat experiments, and we learned about how motors make electricity. It was cool to talk about that with my dad since he deals with motors all the time. It's the only class I got an "A" in for all four quarters this year.

I don't know what my favorite subject will be next year. Probably science again, because I like to know how things work. But maybe not. Mrs. Randello, the math and science teacher, is retiring, and I don't know who the new teacher will be. Maybe I'll end up picking a new favorite subject. After all of this writing, I'll probably be a whiz at language arts.

4. <u>What do you do for fun?</u>

There's the stuff I already told you about, like reading comic books. The comic shop I go to has every series you could think of! My favorite superhero is probably Spider-Man. When he's out of his costume, he takes photos for a living, sort of like my mom does. Plus, Spider-Man is tough and a brave guy, but he's also kind of a big nerd. I don't know why, but I think that's awesome.

The problem is, the comic shop is all the way over in SLO. That's what we call San Luis Obispo. We say it like "slow." There's a word for initials that you say like a word. I want to say <u>acrobat</u>, but that's not it, because acrobat describes Spider-Man.

Sorry...that was my scrambled egg brain again. What I meant to write is, I can't go to the comic shop often. Quin takes me if I ask, but only when Mom and Dad don't need the car. (We only have one car, just like the bathroom.) I'm not allowed to ride my bike that far until I'm older. But that's okay. It's <u>twelve whole miles</u>! I don't have enough muscles to ride that far anyway.

My mom wants to know if I forgot about our movie night. I guess I've been in here for a while. I don't know what gets into me when I write you a letter! I'm going to take a break and work on your last question tomorrow.

All smiles,
Felix Maldonado,
fourth grade graduate

P.S. Remember that big pirate movie that came out a few summers ago? I asked my mom, and they did a scene from that movie in our dunes. It was the part where the pirate king's crew turns against him and he gets stranded on a desert island. Mom had pictures of the set and everything!

P.P.S. The scorpions in that scene were done with computers. We don't have scorpions here. (Luckily!)

June 18th

Dear Lt. Greene,

Today I am not writing to you from my bedroom. Mom got a gig shooting photos at a high school graduation party, so she is gone for the day and she doesn't like leaving me home alone. (Quin had somewhere to be, too, so he could not watch me.) So, I am sitting at a table in the back of my dad's shop. I'm finally ready to answer your last question!

Except it really wasn't a question, was it? It was more like an order.

5. <u>Tell me more about your family.</u>

Sir, yes sir!
(Like in boot camp, get it?)

Dad's family has lived in Pismo since my great-grandparents moved here from the Philippines. (They were immigrants who came here on a ship to follow their dreams.) Mom's family has been here just about as long. Quin got

28

to meet some of our grandparents, but they all passed away before I was born.

I call my parents Mom and Dad. But you are a grown-up, so you would call them Linda and John. Mom and Dad have known each other ever since they were kids. Can you believe that? They went to school together, but they were not boyfriend and girlfriend then, just friends.

Mom left for college to study art, and Dad left for another college. He wanted to be an engineer. But he had trouble and came back before he could finish. He worked as a handyman and fixed cars, and eventually saved up to buy this ATV shop. Mom moved back after she graduated from college, and I guess something was different because they fell in love. They still are, I'm pretty sure. They tease each other about their gray hairs and have private jokes at the dinner table (which is <u>rude</u>!) and they always kiss hello and goodbye. It's disgusting.

But, I know I'm pretty lucky. A lot of my classmates have parents who are divorced or just fight a lot. I try to remember that when kids give me a hard time at school. Mom would call that "looking at the big picture."

Sometimes I wonder if I'm going to end up marrying one of the girls in my class. I mean, you have to get married some time I guess, but I really hope I can meet more people first. It worked out for my parents, but that was just luck, because there isn't a single girl in my grade who is as cool as my mom. I wouldn't even share my lunch with most of them. (Not that anyone asked, ha-ha.)

Anyway, I like my mom. She listens, she's funny, and she's great at taking pictures. Her postcards are so nice; you can't even tell they came from our house and not a card factory. And people are always happy when she shoots their events, like today. The best money is in weddings, but they are the hardest jobs to get because everybody wants them. I think if Mom would just put together a better website, she could make a lot more money.

Mom does other art, too, as a hobby. Lately she's been on this kick where she collects stuff like driftwood and a conch shell and puts it all together into a sculpture. She calls the stuff "found objects," which is art talk for "junk." I don't get it, but I hope someone else does. Like a weird millionaire who wants to decorate his mansion with junky sculptures.

So that's Mom. Dad is not an art person. He says that part of his mind just never got plugged in. But between Mom's creative side and his science side, he jokes that they make up one "really awesome brain." Even though Dad did not finish college, he is smart and is a terrific repairman.

That's good, because it seems like things are breaking all of the time. The ATVs at the shop break because the renters try to go racing and stuff and don't take care of them. Also, they are a little old. (The ATVs, I mean. The renters are mostly young.) Maybe if we have a really busy summer, we will be able to get a new ATV that will not break down for a long time.

Dad is also a bit more of a worrier than Mom. I guess that's where I get it. We both do the same thing when we worry, which is rub the top of our forehead with our fingertips. I hope it does not make me go bald up top like him. He combs his hair differently to cover it, but you can totally tell.

And that's my dad. Now, the only person left to tell you about is Quin. But that will have to wait, probably until Monday. His graduation ceremony is tomorrow, and we're doing family stuff all day.

Your pal of the pen,
Felix

Dear Lt. Greene,

Good news! I talked to my parents, and last night we set up an email address for me! I wrote the address down separately. It's on the back of the business card from my dad's shop. If you don't see the card, check in the envelope. Maybe the paperclip fell off during the trip and it is still in there. And now…

5. <u>Tell me more about your family.</u>
   (Part Two)

Let me tell you about Quin, my older brother. He's eighteen years old and his high school graduation was yesterday. Dad got all teary-eyed and Mom took about a million pictures when he got his diploma.

They were both super proud of him, as you can probably guess. That's because Quin really made a big turnaround. He was not a good student before, but he started taking school seriously and even made the honor roll this year!

Quin is very different from me, and not just because he made honor roll and I didn't. (I got a "C" in math because long division is awful.)

My brother is tall and has big muscles from working out and surfing and drinking protein shakes. He helps out at Dad's shop on weekends. He also just got hired at another place to earn money for college. He'll be waiting tables at a fancy Italian restaurant near the highway. Cal Poly is not cheap, so I hope every customer of his orders lobster and leaves a great tip.

Quin is kind of a daredevil. At least compared to me he is. He loves to try new things and he loves to have adventures. He even surfs at Shark Beach sometimes!

That's a place a few miles north of here. Shark Beach isn't its real name, though, just a nickname. It used to be a popular tourist spot because there were always great waves rolling in. But then, back when I was in first grade, some jetskiers saw a big shark in the water. Nobody got bit, but most tourists still stay away. The taco shack and the surf shop there had to close down.

It's really unfair that those places went out of business because of some dumb shark. But I'll admit, I'm with the tourists on this one. I wouldn't go to Shark Beach either. The warning sign at the shore freaks me out too much. It has a shark and a stick figure on it and says "DANGER." No Shark Beach for this kid!

Anyway, Quin is a pretty good brother. He asks me about school and even helps me with homework and projects if Mom and Dad are busy. He teases me sometimes, like when he told me that the stick figure on the Shark Beach sign looked just like me. (Not true!) But it's different from Roger

Batista and the other kids at school. I guess it's because I know Quin is just joking. Also, I can tease him back because I am not afraid of him. I know he won't hurt me.

We didn't always get along so great, though. I'll put it this way: Batman had the Joker, Superman had Lex Luthor... and until a couple of years ago, I had Quin. He was my <u>arch nemesis</u> (which is like a worst enemy, if you don't read comics).

For a long time, I thought Quin hated me. He didn't like having to share his bedroom with me, that's for sure. He was eight when I was born, so he was pretty used to being an only child.

One time, when I was four, Quin tried to convince me that our bedroom belonged to him only, and that I had to sleep in the closet. I tried it for one night, but I had a bad dream and woke up screaming because it was so dark. After that, Quin said that I could stay in the room...but he told me, "Not because Dad said so. Because I said so!"

Once Quin got into high school, we started fighting less. But it wasn't because we'd gotten closer. It was just that he and my parents were fighting so much that he didn't have time to be mad at me.

You see, by ninth grade Quin had started running with a bad crowd. He goofed off in class and got into all kinds of trouble around the neighborhood. In his junior year, Quin got into the worst trouble of all...the police kind.

Here is what happened. One night, Quin and a couple of his lousy friends took paintball guns and went around shooting people's stuff with them. But only Quin got caught. That was because he had borrowed one of Dad's ATVs to drive everyone around. Someone saw the license plate and the cops were waiting for Quin at our house when he got home.

Quin had to fix a boat that the kids all hit with paint, but its owner did not press charges. It was really lucky that Quin did not have to go to jail or something. He was just grounded for a very long time. Dad was so let down that he wouldn't even talk to Quin for a while.

Maybe that's why Quin and I started talking more around that time. Really talking, I mean, not just arguing. Quin made other changes, too, like dropping his bad friends and working harder in school. In a weird way, I think getting in trouble like that scared him into growing up.

I really look up to Quin now. I just wish he had decided to grow up earlier, and not only because he would have been nicer to me all that time. It's also because his bad grades from early on have kept him from getting scholarships now. Scholarships are like special checks that are used to pay for college. Maybe you had some yourself.

But that is why my brother can't go to Cal Poly in the fall, because of the money. He doesn't complain a lot, but I know it really upsets Quin that he can't go.

So...that's all of your questions. Now you know all about my life. I hope I didn't bug you. I wrote an awful lot. Don't feel like you have to write as much as I did. I know you're really busy. I'll try to wait until I hear from you before I send anything else. Hopefully I'll hear from you through <u>EMAIL</u>!

Your friend,
Felix "Peanut" Maldonado
(in a nutshell, ha-ha)

ENCLOSURE: Card with email address on back.

Dear Lt. Greene,

I know I said I'd wait until I heard from you. But this just could not wait. I can't believe I did not think of this before! This card you are holding is one of Mom's postcards. Pretty nice, huh?

Mom took this picture in the dunes last September. The guy driving the ATV is my dad. He is short in real life, but he looks tall in the driver's seat. Dad wore that helmet for safety, but I think also because of his hair. He doesn't like how the wind blows it around.

They had to try a couple of times to get the picture just perfect. Normally, Dad does not let anybody hit jumps with his ATVs because it is a safety risk. But he is a good driver, and it was just for the picture. Quin and I helped out. It was a great day. It really was kind of like a party for us, just like the card's title says.

I'm out of space, so time to stop. I hope it doesn't annoy the post office lady that I'm writing on the address side of the card. I already bugged her every day last week for a stamp. I didn't have enough allowance to buy a whole book at once.

Happy Independence Day (since that's about when you'll get this),

Felix

ILT Marcus Greene

FOB Ripley

APO AP 09383

Dear Marcus,

Wow, that'll take some getting used to. But thanks for letting me call you Marcus instead of just Lt. Greene. And thanks so much for emailing me! (My tired writing arm says thanks, too.)

I'm glad you liked reading about my family and my life. Sorry that the other guys in your unit gave you a hard time about all of my letters, though. You can tell them that I'm not "some girl," and <u>NO</u>, I don't have a crush on you, and if I ever meet them, I'll beat them up for saying so!!

(Don't tell them that I am actually scrawny and kind of a chicken. Now that I think about it, don't tell them where I live either. Tell them a fake address if they ask.)

Also, sorry that I got mixed up when I made that boot camp joke a couple of letters back. I did not know that "boot camp" is training for the Marines, not the Army. Thanks for correcting me. I hope it did not offend you.

I want to tell you about my summer so far. Mom needs the phone to make a call, though, so I have to get off the computer for now. That's right, we still have dial-up Internet. Our Internet connection is so junky that if Mom found it lying in the street, she'd probably try to turn it into a sculpture, ha-ha.

I shouldn't complain, though. Dial-up Internet is not as good as the Internet at the library, but it's better than no Internet at all. I'll sign on and write another note after dinner.

Your email buddy,

Felix

Hello again Marcus,

I'll just pick up right where I left off. Summer is off to a pretty good start. A whole load of families came in for vacation, which means more customers for Dad. And Mom got to do photos at a few more graduation parties, so we actually have a bit of extra money right now. Dad fixed the air conditioner at home (it is up in the 80s here), and Mom put three hundred dollars into a savings account for Quin. That was to kick off his college fund. She called it a "drop in the bucket." Can you believe that? I'll bet it wouldn't be a "drop in the bucket" if I asked for that kind of cash!

Quin is putting his tips from waiting tables into that account, too. But he isn't earning what he'd hoped, and he always comes home smelling like butter and garlic from all of the meals he serves. He used to love garlicky food, but now he's getting tired of it. He gets a lot of customers who are rude, too. But Quin used a worse word than "rude."

As for me, I haven't done a whole lot. I hang out at Dad's shop sometimes, and he has me do things like clean the lug nuts when he changes a tire. Bo-ring! I like hanging out with

Quin better. One day when he wasn't working last week, he took me to see a movie up in SLO. It was about racehorses! I hope it wins a bunch of Oscars.

We talked about the movie afterward, and I think horses are not just my favorite animals—they are also my favorite athletes. That might sound weird, but when you think about it, you just might agree. Horses don't let anything get them down. They love to run, they're faster than the fastest person, and they always do their best. Horses are never sore losers, they don't talk trash, and they never get greedy or ask to be traded to another team.

So that's why horses are my favorite athletes. Quin said that he will take me to see some real horses some day. That would be the best! I've never seen a horse race, because the nearest racetrack is at least three hours away. (Trust me, I looked it up.)

So now you're all caught up with me. I hope you find time to write back soon, because I have a few new questions! Drumroll...

1. About your rank: You said you are a Lieutenant 1st Class because you did the ROTC program in school. Why did that help? I thought ROTC was just the kids who carry the flag on the field before high school football games.

2. About the mail: You got all of my letters...did you get the postcard yet, too? I was thinking about that postcard a couple of days ago. It came up because I went to the grocer with Mom and saw the post office lady in line at the checkout. I did not say hi, because I think I bugged her by buying all of those stamps one at a time. But she made me think of the postcard.

3. Last, about the time difference: I know that California and Afghanistan are in different time zones. The Internet says that we're almost exactly twelve hours apart. Do you know if you are twelve hours ahead, or twelve hours behind? I hope you're twelve hours ahead. It would be like you're writing to me from <u>the future</u>.

Good night (or, I guess, good morning),

Felix

Dear Marcus,

HAPPY INDEPENDENCE DAY! Since Afghanistan is twelve hours ahead of Pismo, it is midnight on July 4th where you are. I hope that you and your unit have an awesome day. Do you get a break from your missions and stuff? I hope you get to celebrate. If it wasn't for you guys, we probably wouldn't even have a 4th of July.

I am excited for Independence Day. There is going to be a parade in town. ROTC kids will be there, I'm pretty sure. Or should I say, Reserve Officer Training Corps kids! (Thanks for telling me.)

There will also be guys from the Army National Guard. The Guard has a camp up in SLO. It's called Camp San Luis Obispo (not very creative, I know). The Army National Guard is different from the regular US Army, right? I know they help out in California when there are natural disasters. They helped fight a huge forest fire up in Big Sur a couple of years back. And they watch the border down near Mexico— I guess they are on guard, like the name.

Anyway, ROTC and the Guard will be in their nice, clean uniforms and will march in the parade like they do every year. A bunch of other groups will, too. Like the Shriners, who are old men with funny hats who drive tiny, tiny cars. I am not sure what else they do, but I like them.

Dad, Quin, and I are all going to enjoy the fun together. Mom will be away from us part of the time because she is taking parade pictures for the City of Pismo Beach website. But she'll be back with us in time for my favorite part of July 4th. That's the fireworks! They happen at night, right on the pier. If I'm good, maybe Mom'll let me try to take a picture to send to you!

Try to have fun,

Felix

Dear Marcus,

I liked your story about the 4th of July barbecue. You're a great writer. I could just close my eyes and imagine the airfield where you ate. It really made me appreciate that Dad can grill me a burger any night I want.

It's neat how you got to hang out with Air Force pilots and Marines to celebrate. But I'm wondering…why did you call the Marine guys "grunts"? Do they make a lot of noise while they eat or something? And was it <u>really</u> 105 degrees out? Or was that just a way of saying it was very hot?

Either way, I'm glad you guys got to have a day where you had fun and were sort of safe. You deserve it. Now, let me tell you about <u>my</u> Independence Day!

Sometimes it gets foggy in Pismo, especially near the beach. But yesterday was a bright blue, clear day. Dad closed his ATV shop for the holiday, so he got to go around with Quin and me. We rode our bikes over to the Promenade. That's that bunch of stores near the pier I told you about. Dad and Quin ride faster than I usually do, but I kept up okay. I had my inhaler, though, just in case.

The Promenade is a pretty cool place. It's paved nicely and it overlooks the beach. And there are tall palm trees planted outside every few shops. A lot of the kids from school hang out over there to play pool or video games at the arcade. But I stay away from those places usually. That's because I spend my allowance on things like comics (or stamps!).

Okay, that's not the real truth. You're my friend, and friends should be honest. I really stay away because of rotten Roger and his buddies. They push me around some in school, but they might really beat me up out of school where there are no teachers who will suspend you for fighting.

But anyway, I was with Quin and Dad, so I knew those kids wouldn't try anything even if they saw me. We went and checked out the sights at the Promenade. There were tent booths set up for all kinds of different groups. And, there were stands with all kinds of carnival foods! Dad ate a giant cotton candy. Quin bought me a *churro*. You might not have churros in Kansas. It's like a doughnut, but one that someone straightened out into a stick shape and made extra delicious.

After we got our snacks, we went to the different stages on the Promenade and watched groups perform. There were bands, dancers, and a clown show. (I don't like clowns.) One group was an Asian pride group from Cal Poly. They did a traditional Filipino dance! (The Philippines count as part of Asia, if you did not know.) The girls carried these big round hats and the boys danced around them, mostly while hopping on one foot. Quin did a funny imitation of their dance moves, but I thought the show was cool.

Then came the parade. It wasn't like the Thanksgiving parade on TV or anything, because we're a pretty small place. But the bands played really well. Everyone passed so close to the crowd that people who were friends could high five as they went by. I waved to the ROTC kids for you!

One thing happened that I thought was weird at first. It was when the Army National Guard guys marched by. Dad left to get me a soda when the Guard came by, so it was just Quin and me. Quin didn't make jokes about them like he did about the other groups. He started telling me all kinds of things about the Guard instead. It matched the stuff you told me, like how the US Army and the National Guard are separate, but you do your basic training together. He said that the National Guard is the only part of the military that fights in wars but also helps out in America, too.

I guess it wasn't so weird in the end. After the parade, Quin went and shook hands with one of the National Guard guys. They must be friends, so I guess that's how he knew all of that stuff.

Dad came back a little later, and then Mom joined up with us. She had folding chairs in the car trunk for us to watch the fireworks. We set them up on the Promenade wedged closely together because of how crowded it was. And good news! Mom let me use her camera and tripod to take a picture for you!

Mom helped me with the settings because it's hard to get the f-stop and the aperture right without lots of practice. They work like your eye, but it's hard because your eye does everything on its own, but you have to tell the camera what to do. I lined up the tripod and snapped the picture all by myself.

I attached the picture I took. I'm proud of it, and so was Mom. She liked how I showed my family, but with the pier and the crowd all lit up in the background. She said the picture was "postcard perfect."

Be safe and drink lots of water,

Felix

Dear Marcus,

I'm glad you liked my photo. Maybe I will take some more later in the summer and send them to you. You could probably use some nice stuff to look at besides sandstorms.

It sounds like you are working really hard on your unit's new project. I don't think I'd go anywhere if I had to build the road there first! But I guess it is good that you are building roads between those tiny villages. Do you guys ever get a coffee break when you are building a new road? That is important if you are a construction worker, I think.

It was good timing that you wrote to me about building roads. It made me think of something that happened earlier today.

I was at the shop with Dad and Quin when this real pain in the behind came in. He was not a lot older than you or Quin. But he was huge...I mean built like the Hulk! He was just brownish-red from sunburn instead of green. The only thing that kept him from being totally scary was his face. It was red, like the rest of him, except for these pale white rings around his eyes from his sunglasses. He looked like a raccoon, only with the light and dark parts backward.

From the moment the guy came in, I knew he'd be trouble. I could hear his voice from all the way in the back of the shop. (I was busy sweeping up the sand that people track in on their flip-flops.)

It was weird. The man didn't even seem like he really wanted to rent an ATV. He just wanted to complain and push my dad around. Some people are like that, I guess.

First, the man said that our equipment was not nice enough to charge so much, and he wanted a special discount. When Dad wouldn't give him one, he made Dad come out into the parking lot where we keep the ATVs. Then the guy pointed out every dent on each one, and he said they weren't even the fastest kinds. He said we should be embarrassed. I knew I was right then. All of the other customers could hear this guy, and he was insulting our shop and acting like a bully to my dad.

But Dad stayed so calm. He just listened and said polite things like, "I see," and, "I don't know what to tell you, sir." If I had been in his place, I'd have been shaking in my shorts. Or maybe I'd have busted out laughing...the guy looked really silly with his raccoon tan lines.

Quin wasn't calm or scared or laughing. He was angry. He didn't say anything because my dad told us never to talk back to a customer, but

I could see Quin thinking about it. The whole time, he stood behind the cash register, stiff as a surfboard. He kept clenching his jaw like he was chewing back a bunch of swear words.

In the end, Dad told Raccoon Guy, "If you don't like the selection, you can always take your own car and drive it onto the beach."

That's true; it's legal to do that on a special strip of the beach. You just have to follow the speed limit and yield and stuff. Raccoon Guy said that's just what he was going to do. He had Dad draw him a little map and tell him where the beach ramp was for regular cars.

But there was one little thing Dad left out. Car tires are different from ATV tires. They're thinner and bite deeper into the sand. That's because they are harder from having more air in them. If you don't let some of the air out before you drive onto the beach, your car will sink down and get stuck. And don't even think about speeding up to drive out. The faster you spin your wheels, the deeper you'll sink, and the whole time the volleyball girls who play nearby will just laugh their heads off at you.

And that is exactly what I saw when I rode down to the car ramp on my bike. Raccoon Guy was spinning his tires in the sand and yelling for someone to call a tow truck. The volleyball girls just made an O with each hand and held them in front of their faces, making raccoon eyes.

I think that was Dad's way of getting revenge on that guy for treating him badly. I was worried about it, though. What if Raccoon Guy came back and wanted to fight?

Anyway, that was my very long way of showing that I understand why you need to make the roads in the desert. Maybe if folks didn't get stuck in the sand as much, there would be less anger and fighting.

By the way, please thank your friend Sgt. Shaunessy for sharing his Internet connection with you. I did not know that soldiers had to buy their own Internet hookup. If you want, I can mail you some of my allowance to chip in for the cost.

Write back soon,

Felix

DATE: Mon., Jul. 11 at 6:01 a.m.

SUBJECT: Weird Talk

Hello Marcus,

It's still dark, but when I take a breath I can feel that it will be a foggy day. They're not so great for my asthma, so I have to be careful.

I am the first one up in the house today. You are probably eating dinner now. I hope you are having a fresh, healthful meal and not those nasty Meals Ready to Eat you told me about. They sound even grosser than that freeze-dried stuff the astronauts eat. (By the way, why are they called MREs and not Ms RE?)

I'm surprised that I got up so early. Quin kept me up late in our room talking last night. He was in a terrible mood. I wanted to just get to sleep, but it makes me feel important when he talks to me about real things, so I stayed up and listened instead.

Remember that story I told you about that customer, Raccoon Guy? That's what we talked about. Quin was still angry about it, all those hours later! But the weird thing was, he didn't sound too mad at Raccoon Guy. He was really mad at Dad. He was upset that Dad didn't stand up to the guy and toss him out of the store.

"He just lets people treat him like dirt," Quin said. "That guy could've wiped his shoes off on

Dad's face and he'd have just said, 'My pleasure to help, sir!'"

(I don't think he meant that for real. Quin is just very descriptive when he is mad.)

I tried to tell Quin about how Dad let the guy get stuck in the sand, and how funny it was to watch. But Quin didn't see it the way I did. He was ashamed of Dad. He said Dad was just chicken and couldn't act like a real man.

There was a lot more Quin complained about, like college, and how he can't go, and how Dad never finished and that's why he's stuck at that shop forever.

I tried to argue back at first. Even though Dad worries sometimes, I think he likes our life, and so do I most of the time. But nothing got through to Quin. I finally gave up and said I needed to get to sleep.

But Quin had one more thing to say. I remember the last thing he told me. His voice got low and his lip got quivery and he whispered, "I'm getting out of here, Felix. One way or another I'm getting out."

It made me nervous to hear Quin talk like that. He hasn't sounded like that in a long time, not since he was a troublemaker who was always fighting with our parents. He used to tell me that he was going to stow away on a ship and go far away and make them sorry.

It's awful, but back when he'd say that stuff, I'd get to thinking, "Stop whining and go do it already!" But I like Quin now. I don't want him to turn back into the old bad Quin. I don't want him to disappear.

I feel better now that I wrote all this down. It's been a big help having you as my pen pal. Maybe I'll go back to bed and get a little more sleep before breakfast.

Your tired friend,

Felix

Dear Marcus,

Thanks for getting back to me. I think you're right. Quin was just blowing off steam. He seems better now. He promised to take me over to SLO before work today so that I can get a new comic book. (I will do what you said and use my allowance on myself.)

I just wondered: Do you ever read comics? Or does anyone else in your unit read them? I could mail the one I buy today to your base when I finish it. That way I am using my allowance on "me," but not only on me. You don't have to answer right away. I know that you are busy with your road project.

Hope you're feeling great,

Felix

Marcus,

Quin's gone crazy. He ran out of the house and Mom and Dad are really upset. Everything is so messed up.

It all started when Quin came home early for dinner. We were surprised. Mom only made enough chicken for three people, because Quin was supposed to be at work until late. She asked why he was home early, and Quin said he'd quit his job. Dad began to scold him for just walking out of his job, because that is irresponsible. But then things got way worse, because Quin told Dad why he quit.

Quin signed up to join the Army National Guard. He can't keep his job because he has to leave for Basic Training in a couple of weeks.

That kicked off the worst argument I've ever seen my family have. Mom was upset that Quin hadn't talked to them first. But Dad totally blew up. He yelled and stood up so fast that he hit a glass on the table and broke it.

Quin said he had been thinking about join- ing for a while now. He said the Guard will give him money to pay for college. Dad yelled that he was being foolish. Quin yelled back and called Dad a quitter for not finishing school. It got so scary. I thought they were really going to really fight, like the punching kind. Mom was worried about that too, because she sent me to my room. I was really glad to go. I hate when I cry in front of Dad or Quin.

Mom took charge and ordered both of them to calm down and talk things out. The shouting stopped, but I could still hear Quin from our bedroom. He said that he is an adult and he has made a choice, and Mom and Dad better just accept it. Then Quin went out for a walk even though Dad told him to stay.

I could hear Mom and Dad talking after, but they were too quiet for me to hear what they were saying. When they finished, Dad came in to the bedroom. He was embarrassed for losing his temper in front of me. He said he was wrong to do that, but he was just so shocked. Then he said, "We'll figure everything out. Don't worry."

But <u>HOW</u> am I supposed to not worry? Quin is smart and strong, but he's not a soldier like you. He wouldn't be careful. I am very confused and I need your advice. Please help me. What should I tell Quin to make him change his mind? Can you maybe talk to him?

Thank you,

Felix

Dear Marcus,

I guess you didn't get my last email yet. I know it has only been three hours, but I was hoping I would get lucky. Quin is still out and my parents are up waiting for him to get back. They think I am asleep (yeah right).

Please, please write back the moment you get this.

Felix

You aren't hurt are you? I had a thought that you were hurt or might be in danger, and that was why you hadn't written back. Now the worry won't leave my head. Please don't be hurt. I need your help.

Dear Lt. Greene,

I'm very sorry for getting all weird. I did not mean to make you uncomfortable. I understand that you are very busy, and that you are not just sitting around waiting for me to write you. I get it, really.

You are right that this stuff with Quin is a family thing. I should not have asked you to get in the middle of it. I should probably do what you said and talk to my parents first when I get very upset. It's just that they were upset, too, and I felt like they couldn't help me. Still, I will try to talk to them first next time.

But I still want to be your friend. I know that I am a lot younger than you and we have never even met. But you are fun to hear from and easy to write to. I will be more patient and not a pest or a burden, I promise. I hope I did not make you stop wanting to hear from me.

Your friend (I hope),

Felix

P.S. Just so you know, Quin did come back after my last email. He really is joining the National Guard. He can't back out even if he wanted, he says, because he signed the papers to "enlist." I guess that's like a contract.

Dear Marcus,

Thanks for sending me a note and checking in. I appreciate your thinking of me. I have been thinking of you, too.

I'm still worried about Quin, but I am feeling less panicked. Mom and Dad are better, too. They've been talking with Quin a lot, and they are trying to give him support. They can tell that he has thought a lot about his choice.

Here is what I have learned so far. Quin leaves for Basic Training in a few weeks, right before I start fifth grade. He says that we will have something in common: we will both be students. I guess that was supposed to be a joke.

Quin's "school" is shorter than mine, but not by a whole lot. That's because he has Basic Training for ten weeks, and then he has something called Advanced Individual Training after, where he'll learn a special skill. That could be short or long depending on what skill he picks.

But I guess I don't really have to tell you all that, do I, <u>Lieutenant</u>? (Ha-ha.)

I want to just be proud of Quin. He will be serving his country in the Guard, and he wants to go to college to make something of himself after. But...there's the war. What if he ends up out there?

Quin says, "Don't worry so much." That's what everybody says. Like I could just blink my eyes and forget.

Still, I'm trying to take the advice. Yesterday, I rode over to the cliffs near the Batista hotel and listened to the ocean. It was clear out when I started the ride over, but by the time I got there the fog had rolled in really thick. I couldn't see the waves crashing. I couldn't see the pier or the tourists that look like tiny ants.

I got mad about it at first. I thought about all of my mom's postcards with their perfect weather—but it's foggy almost half the time and she never takes a picture of that. Things are never really as nice as they are on a postcard.

But then I looked back at the fog and had a new thought. Everybody down on the pier was stuck in the fog, too. Everyone in the fog was just like me, with no idea what was happening down the way.

I guess that's a weird thought for a kid to have. I'm only supposed to be worried about my grades and what I'll get for Christmas. There probably isn't another kid in Pismo Beach who feels like I do.

Still, I think sitting at the cliffs for a while helped, because that sick feeling I've had in my stomach went away. For a little while, anyway.

Write when you can,

Felix

Dear Marcus,

Thank you for telling me some facts about how Basic Training works. The more I know about what is happening, the less nervous I feel. Do you really think Basic will turn Quin from just a normal smart guy to a real soldier like you? I hope it does. I mean, I love my brother, but look at him. Does he really look like soldier material?

You know, it's kind of funny. He wants to go to college so that he won't get pushed around like Dad. But first, he's going to do nothing but get pushed around. He'll have to follow every order he gets, no matter what he thinks, won't he?

I guess Quin is learning all of that right now. He is off at a special class over at Camp San Luis Obispo. The class is supposed to get Quin ready for Basic Training. They'll teach him the ranks in the Army National Guard and how not to make his drill sergeant mad. (Quin will probably need a lot of help there, ha-ha!) I guess it is like practice Basic Training. He is over at Camp SLO a lot.

(I was just thinking, Camp SLO sounds kind of funny doesn't it? Like a camp for senior citizens or something.)

I am trying not to "obsess" over things, to use your word. Because you are right—I think it is driving me crazy to be so afraid. Quin is making a tough choice in joining the National Guard, and I should show respect and be strong.

I think I thought of a way to be strong. Maybe I can find something in my life that scares me and try not to be scared of it anymore. Kind of like how you were scared to fly in a plane, but then you had to get over it when it was time to fly to Afghanistan.

(Believe it or not, I am not scared of flying in a plane one bit. But maybe that's because I've never flown before.)

Your crazy young friend,

Felix

Dear Marcus,

Today, I did just like I said. I faced one of my fears. Not a big one, but it was a start. I decided to stop being such a chicken and go hang out at the Promenade. After all, it doesn't belong to Roger Batista and his friends. I should be able to play there just like any other kid.

I took four dollars of my allowance, told Mom where I was going, and rode my bike over. I locked my bike up on a bench near the surf shop where Quin buys his board wax. And then I went to the video game arcade. And do you know what happened to me when I got there?

I had <u>FUN</u>! I played Skiball and hit the 100-point hole not once, but twice. I did a motorcycle racing game where you have to lean to steer. The only game I stayed away from was that Bell of Liberty army shooting game. I didn't want to play it. Do games like that bother you? Or do you like them since you cannot get hurt?

There was one time where I got nervous. It was when I was trading in my Skiball tickets for one of those cheap plastic prizes (I got a lip balm with a picture of a horse on it). While I was in line, I saw two kids from school come in, Lupe and Kenneth. They are friends with

Roger, but he was not with them. It was funny, because I thought they would try to take my quarters or push me like they do in school, but they didn't. They gave me a quick look and just passed by to play air hockey. I wonder if it's really just Roger who is the problem and his friends just go along.

Once I ran out of money, I went back home and helped peel carrots for dinner. It was a good day. The only thing I wish is that I could have tried to be brave earlier. It worked out great! But there are only a few weeks left in the summer. Now I just have to find a way to double my allowance so I can play more.

Thanks for your advice,

Felix Maldonado

Skiballer 1st Class

Dear Marcus,

Get it? I have more information about Quin. Quin-formation!

Anyway, I finally got a chance to talk to Quin this morning because it is Saturday and he does not have any classes.

I hung out with him and asked him questions while he mixed up his morning protein shake. Quin told me how it is going to work when he ships out for Basic Training next week. It's hard to believe it is only one week away.

"I have to start down in LA," he said. (Los Angeles.) "That's where the MEPS is. You want some of this?"

He meant the protein shake. I said, "No way!"

"You sure?" he asked. "I put an extra raw egg in it."

I pointed to my throat and gagged, which made him smile. I like making my brother smile.

"What's MEPS, anyway?" I asked. That was something you and I had not talked about.

So Quin told me how the MEPS is a big building where soldiers go to get sworn in. "There's a ceremony where I say the oath," he explained. "But before that, the officers there will give me a physical and one final test before they send me off, just to make sure I'm not a total dummy or a wacko."

"So it'll be pretty hard for you to pass, huh?" I asked.

Quin faked like he was going to punch me. I knew he'd pull back, so I only flinched a little bit. He chuckled and then chugged some of that gross shake.

"Do you know where you're getting shipped?" I asked.

"Place called Fort Benning," he said, wiping his mouth. "It's way down south in *Georgia*." (He did an accent and called it *Jawww-gia*.)

I couldn't believe he'd have to train all the way across the country! "How on earth are you getting there?" I wondered. I was pretty sure that Mom and Dad wouldn't pay for the trip.

And Quin looked at me all serious and said, "I'm a soldier now. I have to hike there."

My jaw must've dropped far enough to fit a whole fist in my mouth. Quin busted up laughing.

"I'm just messing with you," he said. "They fly me out. I have to get myself down to LA, and the Guard will fly me to Atlanta. Then it's a bus to Benning, where I'll do Basic. Then, for the next part, I get shipped over to Virginia for eight weeks. And then I come back home to serve."

I had an answer to that, but I didn't say it. I didn't want to be negative and say he might have to go somewhere else.

"You coming?" Quin asked.

"To Georgia?"

"No, Peanut-head, out to the beach!" he replied. "It's my last chance to surf for half a year! I'm going up to hit Shark Beach."

As you could probably guess, I stayed behind. I want to be braver, but I still have my limits.

I'm glad I wrote all of my talk with Quin down. The closer we get to his date to leave, the more I want to pay close attention to everything he and I do together.

Be safe and secure,

Felix

Dear Marcus,

I'm wondering…Quin says that the moment he takes the National Guard Oath, he stops being a surfer and starts being a soldier. Is that really how it works? I still can't picture him that way.

I'll have to get used to the idea soon, though. Quin's swearing-in ceremony is in only five days. Mom is going to drive Quin down, and I get to come with her! Mom said I will be good company, especially since Dad can't come. He can't close up the shop on a Friday, not during summer.

It's too bad Dad has to miss such an important day. But there is one plus side to it. Mom said that since Dad won't be with us, we don't have to rush right back home the same day. She told me, "If you can find something fun for us to do, we can spend the day. We'll sleep over at Aunt Janine's and drive back the next morning."

Aunt Janine is Mom's older sister. She lives in a city called Burbank, California. They film a lot of TV shows there, but she does not work for TV. She owns a beauty parlor, which is funny, because I don't really think Aunt Janine does her hair or makeup very nice. Maybe she does it better on other people.

I hope Dad really is staying behind for the shop, and not because he and Mom are in a fight. Dad has been less patient and more snappy lately. He has been rubbing that worry spot on his forehead a lot. I want to help him feel better. But if he wanted my help, he would probably ask, right? Like when I have to fetch his tools for him.

Think good thoughts,

Felix

Dear Marcus,

So I've been searching online for something fun to do in LA for a boy and his mom. I didn't find a lot of choices, unless you call driving around in a bus and looking at movie stars' houses fun. Some people like that, I guess. But I wouldn't care to see a movie star's house unless I knew he would be out front mowing the lawn or washing his limousine or something.

I was getting frustrated, but then I remembered something I'd looked up earlier in the summer. I couldn't believe I had forgotten about it. There is a famous racetrack near Los Angeles. So...I talked to Mom, and she is going to take me to a horse race!

I am glad to have something I can look forward to. Now, August 12th is not just the day when Quin leaves us for months and months. It is also the day I will get to see a real live horse, up close and in action! Those two things don't balance out all the way, but it helps.

By the way, have you ever been to a horse race? I am asking because I know that a lot of people gamble on the races. Will I have to make a bet? I will try it if that's the rule, but I would rather just enjoy the race and not worry who will win.

Your number one pal-omino,

Felix

P.S. Palomino is a kind of horse. I don't know if you knew that.

Hi Marcus,

Thanks for answering my question about horse races. But I am sorry to say, it doesn't matter now anyway. I will not be going to a horse race after all.

We are skipping the racetrack because it will not just be Mom and me anymore. Dad decided at the last minute to close the ATV shop for the day and come along after all. I don't know why he changed his mind, but he did. That means that we will have to drive back tomorrow night and not stay over. Dad needs to be back Saturday for the shop.

I don't know why I'm so mad at Dad for changing our plans. It's very selfish of me. It will definitely be better for Quin if Dad comes and we all say goodbye as a family. He's really happy Dad is coming along.

I'm not going to grouch anymore. Quin is cooking us a nice pasta-and-clams dinner—it's a recipe he "borrowed" from his restaurant job. Can you believe that? It's Quin's last night here, and he's cooking us dinner. He even picked the clams himself, just south of Grand Avenue while the tide was in.

I won't be able to write tomorrow since we'll be driving down to Los Angeles and back, but I'll tell you all about the trip on the 13th.

Trying to be good,

Felix

P.S. Dad better not make us listen to that lousy jazz music he likes the whole ride. That's all I'm going to say. You can't even hum along to it.

Hi Marcus,

I was going to wait until the daytime to write about our trip, but I am having trouble sleeping. I don't like having my own room. I used to think I would like it, because Quin's nose whistles a little when he sleeps. But now it's just too quiet. I've been hoping a freight train might go by on the tracks near our house so that the rumbling could lull me to sleep, but no luck.

So here I am, writing to you. The one good thing about writing this late is that no one will need the phone in the middle and I can take my time. I am sorry if this note gets too long.

Yesterday, we left for Los Angeles. It was a three-hour drive. We had to fit Quin's bag in the trunk and get on the road before the sun was even up.

It was a quiet ride, quiet like my room. Dad did not make us listen to jazz. He did not want to talk very much. He said he wanted to focus on driving. And Quin slept most of the way down. The car window made a funny red splotch on his temple from how he was resting his head.

Once the sun started to rise and we could see better, Mom challenged me to a round of the alphabet game. That's a game where you read the signs and bumper stickers you pass. You try to find words on them that start with each letter of the alphabet. Whoever gets from A to Z first wins. It's a lot of fun, except when it's time for Q and X words. One of us usually tells Quin he'd better jump out the window so we can use him for Q. But no one made that joke today.

Los Angeles looks very different from Pismo. The best way to describe it is that LA is very <u>new</u> looking. It's all metal and glass and concrete. Even the freeway is concrete, not pavement. Pismo does not look new at all. The sand sweeps all over the place and makes the whole town look kind of dusty.

We arrived at the MEPS right on time. It was bigger than I thought it would be. Quin says the MEPS in Los Angeles is the biggest one in the country. I thought it would have camouflage colors, but it just looked like a really nice college building.

When we got in, Quin had to go off on his own to take his physical and other tests. We had to wait in the waiting room for a really long time while he did that.

We had lunch at the cafeteria and Mom said I could get whatever I wanted. So I had a piece of fried chicken and three pudding cups. (They were fresh and not runny at all.) After lunch, a soldier came and got all of the waiting families. Quin and the others were done with their tests. It was time for them to say the Oath and become soldiers.

All of the families went into a big room. It had wood panels on every wall, like the hunting and bait shop where Dad gets his fishing gear. One wall had a bunch of flags along it. There were no chairs, so we stood in the back. I was under a framed photo of some general or other very important soldier.

Once the families were in place, an officer in his full uniform led the new soldiers in. I couldn't believe how many kids there were besides Quin! It must have been a pretty good day for the recruiters. Everybody marched in, standing tall. Quin winked at me as he passed by.

Maybe that was what set me off. I don't know. All I know for sure is that just as the Oath began, I started feeling horrible. My chest got tight and I couldn't get my breath, like when I ran too hard in gym class and had an asthma attack. I wanted my inhaler, but it was in Mom's purse because I was wearing dress slacks and it looked funny in my pocket.

Some things that aren't very interesting happened next. So I will skip ahead to the end and let you know that I am fine. I calmed down and did not use my inhaler after all.

Mom said Quin did his Oath exactly right. So, my goofball brother is now Private Quin Maldonado, US Army National Guard. Let me tell you, that is weird to type.

I think I am finally getting tired again, so I'd better wrap up. After everyone was sworn in, it was time to say goodbye. Quin starts Basic Training on Monday, so he had a flight to Fort Benning that night. We said our goodbyes in the MEPS waiting room.

When Quin talked with me, he did not just say goodbye. He also gave me a present. It was an envelope. He said, "Don't open this when you get home. And don't open it if you just miss me."

"So when do I open it?" I asked.

He told me, "Open it on the worst day of your life."

I love my brother, but he is even weirder than me sometimes! I wanted to ask him what he meant, but then he rubbed the top of my head and said, "I love you, Felix."

And I didn't want to ask anything else.

Feeling a little better,

Felix

P.S. When it was time to drive home, we stopped to fill up the gas tank. I saw a postcard at the convenience store and thought of you. It has a great picture of Los Angeles on it. I will mail it tomorrow.

Dear Marcus,

I should be honest. In my email about MEPS day, I skipped over a part. It was during the Oath ceremony. I didn't write it because I was ashamed. I said I felt like I was having an asthma attack, and then I made it sound like it just went away.

But that was a lie. The truth is, I lost it. Like a big, loud baby. I got the hiccups from trying to hold the tears in. I felt like I might drown. Dad pulled me out of the room before I wrecked the whole ceremony. He whispered something to Mom and he scooped me right out into the hall. But he didn't scold me for making a scene. Dad said, "It's okay, Peanut. Breathe with your belly. It's okay." And we stayed out in the hall, just breathing, my stomach puffed out like a pot belly. It looked silly, but it worked. I guess it was not an asthma attack after all.

Dad usually lets Mom handle this kind of stuff. But he was perfect. I just feel awful that he missed Quin's Oath because of me. I'm worried that Dad will regret it and blame me. And I'm worried I gave Quin bad luck. But I'm most worried that you will read this and not want to be email buddies with a boy who cries. You won't get this postcard for two weeks, though. Maybe if I am extra brave before then, I will make up for being such a wimp. Deal?

I will try hard,

Felix

ILT Marcus Greene
FOB Ripley
APO AP 09383

Dear Marcus,

I was really in the mood to go buy a comic book today. Wednesdays are when the new issues always come out. But Dad is at the shop (like always) and Mom is working on an art project (another junk sculpture).

I really did not want to hang out in my room or visit the shop. Since my allowance has been "burning a hole in my pocket," to use a Quin quote, I went back to the Promenade and played at the arcade.

I did not do so great at Skiball today. My hand wouldn't throw where my brain wanted the ball to go. But something else happened today that was pretty neat.

I saw those kids I told you about, Lupe and Kenneth. It was just the two of them again, no Roger. They were back to play more air hockey. They gave me a nod as they walked past me to the table. And then, I decided to do something totally not like the usual me.

I walked over and asked Lupe and Kenneth if I could play air hockey with them. It could be like a tournament. They looked at me like I was an alien at first, and I thought that I'd made a big mistake.

But Lupe shrugged and said, "We go first, then you play the winner."

And that's what we did. Lupe and Kenneth love real hockey, but there is no ice rink around here to play, so they settle for air hockey. They know the names of all the pro hockey players. I didn't know who they were talking about most of the time. But we are all excited about the hockey movie that is coming out around Christmas, so we have that in common.

We kept going around, with each new game being the winner of the last game versus the kid who had been sitting out. The final score was Lupe with nine wins, Kenneth with five wins, and me with only two. But since I'd never played air hockey before, I think I did pretty great! Lupe and Kenneth wanted to play more, but I ran out of quarters.

After our first few games, I asked the guys why Roger was not hanging out with them. They said he's been away all summer! He was away at some summer camp, and after that he went traveling with his mother. He won't be back until right before school. I was so annoyed with myself. All this time I'd been hiding from someone who wasn't even there.

I wonder if Lupe and Kenneth are my friends now. I am not sure, but I don't think you are supposed to just come out and ask. I hope they are. I would like to have some company when that hockey movie comes out.

By the way, congratulations on finishing that road project! What will you be doing next?

I hope you are well,

Felix

Dear Marcus,

Sorry that I have not written in a week. I have been busy with a bunch of back-to-school things. I shopped with Mom for notebooks and other supplies. On another day, we got some clothes at the thrift shop. I had hoped we could get something nice and new, maybe as an early birthday present. A very early birthday present. I turn eleven on November 20th, by the way... hint, hint! (Totally kidding.)

Anyway, Mom did not let me buy any brand-new clothes. Mom said that when I am in high school, it will be very cool to get old clothes from the thrift shop. Well, last time I checked, I will not be in high school next week. I will be in fifth grade!

I've also been busy for fun reasons. By that I mean that I played with Lupe and Kenneth three more times this week. I am getting better at air hockey, but Lupe is still the best of us three.

To earn money, I helped Dad reorganize all of the shelves at our shop. I asked Mom to give me a job, too. She had me go hunting for a bunch of different supplies that she could use for sculptures. That was a really tough job, because the only instructions she gave me were to "use my imagination." I really can't tell the difference between a "found object" and plain garbage. But she gave me five dollars for that, too! I guess I did an all right job.

I have been thinking a lot about that envelope that Quin gave me before he left. Not because I've had "the worst day of my life," but just because he told me not to open it…which really makes me want to open it. Maybe it is a gift certificate to the comic shop.

I've been thinking about Quin a lot. He said that we would not hear from him for a while, because the rules at Basic Training are very strict. I am just curious what he has learned now that he has finished a whole week. What did you learn during your Basic Training, Week 1?

Your curious friend,

Felix

P.S. I really was joking about the present thing. Your being my friend is a great gift already. When is your birthday?

Dear Marcus,

I don't have a lot of time to write because I have to get an x-ray and a tooth cleaning at the dentist. I had a checkup at the doctor yesterday. He said that even though I am skinny, I am not so thin that it is a problem for my health. I hope the kids at school will agree this year.

Anyway, thanks for telling me about the first few weeks of Basic Training. It's neat... my brother is getting his soldier training in Georgia. And at the same time, all the way over in Afghanistan, you are starting your new job of training the Afghans to be soldiers. It made me think of some new questions. (I'm sure you expected that, though. You know me pretty well by now.)

Here are the questions:

Do you give the Afghans the same training you learned in America, or is it different?

Do you teach them in English, or did you have to learn the language of Afghanistan? (I do not know what it is called, sorry!)

If you do an extra good job training the Afghans, do you get to come home sooner?

Thanks for being patient with all of my silly questions. I hope the answer to the third one is "yes."

Fingers crossed,

Felix

Dear Marcus,

I was wrong. I hate the Promenade. I hate Lupe and Kenneth. And most of all, I hate that rotten Roger Batista. It's wrong to hate somebody, I know. But I mean it, and they deserve it.

I was hoping I'd feel better by just typing that, but I don't yet. So I guess I'll tell you the whole lousy story. Here is what happened.

I had plans to meet Lupe and Kenneth at the arcade. We were going to hold the World Air Hockey Championship. (That is not a real thing with a trophy. That was just our name for it.)

I spent all morning earning up money for the championship. I helped Dad change a tire, and I cleaned the bolts that held it on with a chemical called tetra-something. Then I stood in our little parking lot and replaced the flags that go on the backs of all the ATVs. They are neon colors and go on thin metal flag poles that screw into the back bumpers. They're really tough to unscrew because sand works its way into the threads.

Once I had earned eight dollars, I rode my bike all the way over to the arcade. It was even more crowded than normal. There were a lot of kids from school. We all wanted to have one last bit of fun before school starts again next week.

Lupe and Kenneth were not there yet, though. I waited for a while, just hanging out because I wanted to save my quarters. But I didn't want to look weird to the other kids, waiting around like that. So I played this old spaceship flying game that is lame, but at least only costs one quarter.

I played through a couple of rounds, and I started to think that maybe Lupe and Kenneth weren't coming. I was upset for a second, but then I had another thought. *This means that they forfeit. I am the Air Hockey World Champion!*

Barely a moment after my brain spat that idea out, I felt this cold, wet stuff hit me in the back. I thought someone had pegged me with an ice cream cone or something. But when I turned around, it wasn't ice cream.

It was Lupe and Kenneth. And mean, jerky old Roger Batista. And they were holding Super Soakers. I shouted at them for spraying me, but they just laughed and zinged me again with that cold water.

I heard my spaceship die behind me, "woop woop woop." Then I noticed the smell. The water they shot on me smelled terrible, like seaweed and rotten fish. My shirt reeked from it.

"What's the matter?" Roger asked. "Don't you like your new cologne?"

I demanded that they tell me what they hit me with.

"Chill out, it's just water," Kenneth said.

"Yeah," Lupe laughed. "Pier water."

I almost threw up right on the spot. I couldn't yank my shirt off fast enough. I pulled it over my head, trying not to get any of that fishy, seagull poopy pier water on my face. And I hollered at the top of my lungs at Lupe and Kenneth for betraying me.

Which was stupid, now that I think about it. If I hadn't yelled, maybe the other kids wouldn't have come around and seen me. By the time I got my dripping shirt over my head, a whole bunch of them had begun to gather.

My shirt hit the floor with a splat.

"Gross," said one girl. "Who stinks?"

"It's Fish Boy!" someone else called out.

Roger laughed. "He's not a fish boy," he said. "He's a fish stick."

Have you ever had the whole world laugh at you? That's what happened next.

I sprinted out to the bike racks and unlocked my bike. My lungs felt like they wouldn't inflate. I hopped on my bike anyway and rode off. I had to get away to some place I couldn't hear the kids calling me "Fish Stick."

There is an underpass near my house where I cross under Highway 101. When I got there, I pulled my inhaler from my pocket and breathed in the vapors from it. And I waited under there in the dark like some troll under a bridge until I felt like I could make it the rest of the way home.

I got home and Mom asked me why I was dirty and where was my shirt. I told her what had happened and she listened, but she didn't have good advice for what I should do. She said that Fish Stick isn't so bad of a name, and maybe I should try talking to Roger and the others. That's what they teach at school, that you should talk to your bullies and tell them how they are hurting you. But I don't think that would work. Roger is just a bad kid, and there's nothing more to say.

If Quin was here, he'd give me good advice. He's older and smarter, but he's not so old that he's forgotten what being a kid is really like. Why'd he have to go and leave me behind?

I thought about opening his mystery letter today after I got home, but I didn't. Partly it's because I'm mad at him. But there was a better reason I decided to save it. That's because I know that today isn't the worst day of my life. That'll be Monday. That's when I start fifth grade.

Not at all excited,

Fish Stick Maldonado

Marcus,

I have to be straight with you. I don't understand your advice. You said that the bravest thing I could do is just go to school on Monday with my head held high. How is that supposed to be brave? I don't have a choice. I have to go on Monday, or I'll get in trouble for being "truant."

And this "holding my head high" business. Do you mean I should just go in and pretend like this weekend didn't happen? If that's your advice, you're a little late. I already got the same story from my dad.

I tried to talk to him last night when he got home, since Mom couldn't help much. Do you know what he told me? Dad's genius advice was to ignore those jerks and focus on school. Mom says talk to them. Dad says ignore them. It's ridiculous.

When he finished giving me his pep talk, Dad put his arm around my shoulders and said I needed to "buck up."

You know what I thought of when Dad said that? I remembered that shop where he buys his fishing lures. They don't just sell stuff for fishing, though. They sell hunting stuff, too, like shotguns to scare off coyotes and rifles for birds and big game. Guess what the owner has hanging on the wall. A twenty-point buck. That buck was big and proud, with great big antlers, and the store owner shot him dead and hung his head on a wall. That's what "buck up" means to me.

You and Dad want me to pretend like Roger and the others don't bother me. But isn't that just lying? It's not brave at all. Couldn't you have given me some real advice, like how to fight? You guys learn how to fight in the Army, you told me. It's Basic Training, Week 2. If it is all right for soldiers to fight, it should be all right for me to fight. If I promised not to really hurt Roger, would you teach me?

One very frustrated kid,

Felix

DATE: Mon., Aug. 29 at 7:12 p.m.
SUBJECT: 1st day
(one attachment)

Dear Marcus,

I want to tell you about my first day of school, but before that I owe you an apology. I reread my last email when I got home. I was disrespectful, and I'm sorry for that. I appreciate your advice, I really do. You've really helped me this summer. I was just in a miserable mood. But I should not have given you attitude. Still friends?

So, being in fifth grade is a lot like being in fourth grade, it turns out. It's basically fourth grade, but with more homework.

And more <u>beards</u>. Last year, all three of my teachers were ladies. This year, two of my three teachers are men, and both of them have beards.

The first beard belongs to Mr. Dulac. He teaches language arts and is my homeroom teacher.

(I don't know if you had language arts back when you were in school. It's just reading and writing with a cooler name. It sounds more important, I think. Like when I graduate, I would be earning my black belt in the language arts, ha-ha.)

Anyway, Mr. Dulac has a short, neat beard and he wore a purple vest to school today. He had us do stretches during homeroom. He said they were to get ready for a year of "reaching for the stars." It was cheesy, but at least he tried to make the day fun.

That's a lot more than I can say for Mr. Cesar. He is my other teacher with a beard. He replaced Mrs. Randello as the teacher for fifth grade math and science.

Even though he is a new teacher, Mr. Cesar is kind of old. He has thick glasses and a great big bushy gray beard. It's the kind of beard you look at and just think, "That thing probably gets a lot of soup caught in it." I was actually excited when I first saw Mr. Cesar. He looked like a mad scientist straight out of one of my comic books. I even drew a cartoon of him so that I could show you what I mean!

But he's not a mad scientist at all. I don't think he's any kind of scientist. Mr. Cesar talks slow and he has a boring voice. Even worse, he gave us a worksheet of review problems for math, and they were mostly <u>long division</u>. Just awful.

Still, that was really the low point of the day. I did not have to deal with Roger much, because he is not in my homeroom this year. (Lucky break!) I only have to see him at lunch. He called me Fish Stick and pinched his nose when I went by, but I held my head high like you said I should. It didn't feel good, exactly, but it wasn't the worst feeling, either.

All right...I took a break from homework to write to you, but now it's time to get back to that long division worksheet. I will be working on it for the "remainder" of the evening, ha-ha.

Your hilarious buddy,

Felix

P.S. Mr. Cesar's beard will <u>get you</u>!!!

Attachment: Mr_Cesar.jpg (92 kb)

Dear Marcus,

I hope everything is all right. You usually write back within a day or two, and it has been three days since I sent that last email. I hope I didn't make you mad when I was rude on Sunday.

Maybe you are just super busy with your training job. I can relate to that. Fifth grade has been nonstop homework! It's still the first week of school, and already we are doing a special project for language arts.

Labor Day is coming up, so Mr. Dulac has us thinking about the jobs and careers around us. We are supposed to think of the people close to us and what they do. Then we have to choose a worker we know and do a presentation about him or her next Tuesday or Wednesday (I am in the Tuesday group).

Mr. Dulac says that we are supposed to make our presentations "come alive" for the class. I think that means bring props in to show. We also have to interview the person we are using for our report.

The only four workers I really know are you, Dad, Quin, and Mom. I guess I could present about my dad's shop, but I don't know. We have to answer questions, and if someone asks how my dad decided to do that for a living, I don't really want to talk about it.

I can't use Quin, either. First, he has not really worked in the National Guard yet. He is still in training. Second, I can't interview him anyway since he is not able to use the phone at Basic.

I think I would like to use you as my example of a worker. You have an interesting career, and I'd feel really proud telling everyone that you are my friend and email buddy. I could print out your emails to me and use them as props for the presentation. I hope you say that it is all right for me to use you.

Let me know,

Felix

Dear Marcus,

I wasted three hours last night on the Internet. You want to know why? I was searching for news stories about your unit. I haven't heard from you in a week now, and I got worried that you got hurt in a battle or something. But I couldn't find anything. So I guess you're not hurt and I worried for nothing. You're just mad at me. You must be. I don't know what else to say, since I have already apologized.

Anyway, I don't have time to keep waiting to hear back, so I've decided to do a presentation about my mom instead of you. I did my interview with her today. She had a photo gig (she did engagement pictures on the beach), but she took time to answer all of my questions anyway.

Mom had a great idea for my presentation, actually. She said the best way to learn about photography is by taking lots of pictures. So, she lent me an older camera of hers and she sent me off to practice for the weekend. I asked about using the new one, but Mom is still making payments on it. "It touches no hands but my own," she said. Anyway, the older camera still works fine, and I can take pictures of whatever I want (except for sunbathers). Best of all, I can also bring the camera to school for my presentation!

It feels really good to be trusted with something important like Mom's camera. And it feels good that Mom cared enough to do my interview right away, and not leave me waiting until the last minute.

That's more than I can say for some people.

Felix

Did you stop writing to me because you got my postcard in the mail? The postcard with the picture of Los Angeles on it? If that's the reason, I am very disappointed in you. I was afraid you'd stop being my friend if I told the truth about my crying, and I guess you proved me right. From now on, I'll keep my tears to myself. I won't waste your time with them, that's for sure.

I hope you have a <u>terrific</u> Labor Day.

Your "friend,"

Felix Maldonado

Dear Lt. Greene,

You might notice that I am writing this email at a time when I should be in school. Don't worry, I'm not sick. I'm just <u>suspended</u>. I got suspended from school today. I'm not even supposed to be using the computer right now. But I am anyway, because I wanted to tell you that this is all your fault.

Today was the first day of our language arts presentations. You could tell which fifth graders were supposed to go today because Mr. Dulac told us to dress nicer than usual for when we present. He said since we were talking about professions, we should look "professional." I wore a blue polo shirt with a little sailboat on it.

I did my presentation in the morning. But that is not why I got suspended. The presentation went great. I talked about my mom and what a photographer does. Then I passed around some prints of pictures I took over the weekend. There was one of my dad flipping pancakes for breakfast, a shot from up near the cliffs, and one I took of some tourists digging for clams on the shore. The kids wanted me to pass the camera around, too, but I did not want anyone to drop it so I kept it. I just pointed to the different parts and said what each did. Everyone was still very interested, though.

I got suspended for what happened at lunch. That's when Roger Batista came to my table. Lupe and Kenneth were with him. Roger must have had to present in his class, too, because he was wearing a brand-new white shirt.

Roger walked up to my table and said, "Hey, Fish Stick. I heard you took some real nice pictures."

I must have still been feeling good about my presentation, because I got smart with him. "Yeah, they were nice," I shot back. "You weren't in them."

Roger slid my lunch tray aside and sat down across from me. "I heard you took one up at my parents' hotel," he said.

"I wasn't at your parents' hotel," I said. "I was on the cliffs."

"That's part of the hotel," Roger said, even though that isn't true. "That means the picture belongs to my family."

I pulled my backpack close to me under my seat. That was where my pictures and the camera were. I hadn't wanted to leave them in class where I couldn't keep an eye on them.

"I want my picture," Roger said.

"No," I snapped, raising my voice. "It is mine!"

"Ooh, look who grew a backbone," Roger said with a wide smile. "Then give me your camera. That's the fee."

I was getting very upset. But I didn't want to have another scene like at the arcade. I got up, grabbed my half-eaten lunch and my bag, and started to walk away with my head high.

But that didn't work at all. Roger, Lupe, and Kenneth all followed me. "Come on, Fish Stick," Roger called out. "I just want to play with the camera a minute! So give it or we'll take it!"

Then I felt Roger grab a strap of my backpack and pull. And I lost it.

I dropped my lunch tray right on the ground with a clatter. I whirled around with a closed fist. I wasn't even sure if I would hit anybody. I just wanted them to let go and not take the camera. I'd never even thrown a punch before, not a real one.

My first real punch turned out to be a pretty good one. It caught Roger square on the nose. He let out a loud "Ooh!" and grabbed his face.

"Fight, fight!" somebody yelled.

I was sure Lupe and Kenneth were going to break me into little pieces. But the fight began and ended with that one punch. "Guys, guys," Roger said. There was a panic in Roger's voice that made them just stop coming for me. We all looked at Roger, and then we saw the blood.

Blood dribbled from both of Roger's nostrils and some red drops fell on his nice white shirt. "You ruined my shirt," he said to me. "You ruined it." I could see from his eyes what was going to happen next. I knew from experience.

Mean, rotten Roger broke down and cried. I couldn't believe it. The tears came flooding out and I stopped being mad at him. I just felt sorry for what I'd done. I didn't know how to make him stop. Neither did Lupe and Kenneth. They wouldn't even look at Roger.

I could see all the kids watching Roger cry, and I had to help him. I grabbed his arm to take him out of the lunchroom. But before I could, two lunchroom monitors came and pulled us apart. They dragged us both to the principal's office.

If you had just gotten back to me, I could have done my project on you. I wouldn't have taken those pictures or brought Mom's camera in, and I wouldn't have gotten in a fight with Roger, or made him cry, or gotten suspended. And I wouldn't feel like a terrible kid.

Here is why I feel terrible. The worst part was not the fight, or the blood, or the meeting

I had with Principal Miller and my mom after. This was the worst part.

Principal Miller made Roger and me stay in his office while we waited for our parents to come get us. His secretary called Roger's father and my mother. We didn't talk or argue while we waited. He held a tissue up his nose and just looked at the ceiling.

Mr. Batista got there first. I'd never met him before. He was tall and stern with a shaved bullet head, tight lips, and a sharp gray suit. I went out to sit by the secretary's desk while Principal Miller met with him and Roger.

When the meeting was done, Mr. Batista opened the door and pulled Roger out of Principal Miller's office. And I mean he almost dragged him. Mr. Batista's face was scarier than a jack-o'-lantern, and he was whispering furiously at Roger. But I heard what he said.

"You're a stupid idiot, you know that?" he told Roger. "I can't believe I have such a stupid, worthless son."

"But, Daddy," Roger interrupted.

"Shut your mouth," Mr. Batista hissed at him. "You moron...I can't stand the sound of your voice."

Roger caught me watching as he passed. But he didn't look at me with any anger. He had this look like a dog that's just been kicked. It was so sad.

I don't care what he's done. A parent should never talk to his own kid like that. I know Mom is very disappointed and Dad will raise his voice and give me a lecture tonight, but I know they'll never tell me that I am stupid. It was the worst thing I've ever seen, and you know what? It really wasn't your fault. It happened all because of me.

Felix

DATE: Thu., Sep. 8 at 6:11 p.m.
SUBJECT: Quin's letter

Dear Lieutenant,

I am still suspended. And you still have not written me back. If you didn't write back after that last letter, though, I guess I really can't count on you anymore.

I thought you should know that I opened the envelope from Quin. He left something very special inside. It was amazing, actually. It's the most caring thing anyone has ever done for me.

And I'm not going to tell you what it was.

For the last time,

Felix Maldonado

September 14th

Dear Marcus,

I just got your letter.

I am a really awful friend. I thought you had abandoned me. I should have known you would not do something like that. I am so sorry that you are hurt. But I am glad that you are safe and out of Afghanistan, and that you are going to be okay.

How did the attack happen? Where were you? What day did it happen? I have tried to look the information up, but I must be searching for the wrong things because I can't find a news story about it anywhere. How bad is your arm hurt? It must have been bad if the Army flew you all the way back to Washington, DC, for your surgery.

Your nurse, Mrs. Hunt, has excellent handwriting, by the way. Please tell her thank you for helping to write your letter to me. I am glad she is taking such good care of you. You need to rest your arm and chest so that the scars will heal and you can get back to full strength. If I had money and knew of any flower shops near your hospital (and I knew it would not make her husband mad), I would definitely get some roses sent to the hospital for her. But I don't and I don't (and I don't), so a boring old "Thank you!" will have to do.

Do they have Internet at the Walter Reed National Military Medical Center? I guess not, if we are back to writing letters. Well, write back as soon as you can. Or I guess as soon as Nurse Hunt has time to help. It made me happy to hear from you. It's been really lonely since Quin is not around and I am still suspended from school until the 21st.

I guess you don't know anything about that, though. A lot's happened since I heard from you last. I have to figure out how to catch you up.

Take things slow, but get well fast!
Felix Maldonado

Dear Marcus,

Thanks (to you and to Nurse Hunt) for writing again. It's okay that you don't want to talk about the fighting in Afghanistan. I do think I'm old enough to hear about it, but I don't want to be pushy.

It was neat to learn more from you about Walter Reed. I never knew that there's a special hospital just for soldiers. It's crazy how big the place sounds. It sounds like its own little city with all those different shops inside. Is there really a flower shop right at the hospital, though? And does Mrs. Hunt <u>really</u> expect me to send her flowers, or was that a joke? Tell her that I really can't. My parents took away my allowance since I punched Roger Batista.

I'll bet that last sentence made your eyes bug out, huh? I'll bet you'd never have guessed that I would fight Roger.

That's why I got suspended. But you'll read all about it in a few days when you are strong enough to leave your room and go use the library's Internet. It's neat that you have your very own library in the hospital. We have public Internet at our library, too.

To be honest, I'm a little worried about you reading all of my emails. You'll have a pretty crowded inbox because of me, and I was not very fair to you in some of my messages. But that was because I thought you were just ignoring me. Please try to keep that in mind.

I am trying to be calmer now that I know what really happened. I am trying not to freak out about how you got hurt. This whole thing just makes me think about Quin a lot. If even great soldiers like you can get hurt, I guess it can happen to anybody.

I did some research while I was home from school these past two weeks.

I looked up a bunch of different Army National Guard units that are based near Pismo Beach and SLO. It took a while, but I was able to make a list. There are some units that are home. But there are some that have been called up and sent off to war. The Guard could call up Quin's unit at any time.

I can't let these worries take over my brain, though. I have to go back to school tomorrow, so I need to leave some room to worry about that, ha-ha.

There has been something that has helped me, though. As I made my list of all of the Guard units nearby, I got to thinking. How many other units have guys in them who are just like Quin? And how many of those guys have little brothers who have all of the same worries I do? I don't want any other kid to have to worry like me…but it helps to think that maybe I'm not all on my own.

By the way, something neat happened when I went to mail your last letter. I went to buy a stamp from the post office lady, and you know what? She remembered me! She asked where I'd been since I bought stamps all those days in a row during the summer and then I stopped coming. I guess she didn't think I was such a pest after all.

Your friend and biggest fan,
Felix

DATE: Fri., Sep. 23 at 4:15 p.m.

SUBJECT: Re: Hello, Felix!
(one attachment)

Dear Marcus,

Welcome back to the 21st century!! I am glad that you are back on email. It's faster to go back and forth, which is great, but it also means that you must be getting better. They wouldn't let you leave your room to visit the library if you were not healing well. How does the stitching from your surgery feel?

Thanks for sending me that picture of your Purple Heart medal! I hope you are proud of it. It's just so sad that you had to get hurt to receive it. But you can always show someone your Purple Heart and they will know that you are a hero.

Also, thank you for being a good sport about all of those emails I sent. You're right...I was pretty "dramatic" in them. Maybe you should get another Purple Heart for putting up with me, ha-ha.

Mom and Dad were pretty upset with me for fighting Roger. But when I told them about what had happened, they could tell that I was just as upset as they were. Dad told me, "You know, it's tough to punish a kid who punishes himself as hard as you do." But they sure did find a way. They took away my allowance for a month, and I couldn't watch TV or movies the whole time I was suspended. At least they let me ride my bike still.

They also helped me take the picture in this email! Mom helped me set the camera on a tripod with a timer to take it. She is "Get," I am "Well," and Dad is "Soon." But you could probably already tell that. Dad wanted me to take a second shot since he wasn't ready, but that was actually what I liked best about it. Anyway, I hope you like it.

My first few days back at school have not been bad. I had to take a couple of makeup tests that I'd missed, since I could not take them from home. I'm worried that my teachers think of me as one of the "trouble kids" now. I feel like they look at me differently since I punched Roger, like they don't fully trust me to behave. I hope I am just imagining that.

I think you're right about Roger. I used to think he was just mean, plain and simple. I guess I never thought about why he acted the way he did. I actually had a weird experience with him this week. It was on Wednesday, which was the first day back for both of us. I was sitting by myself at lunch, off in a corner of the cafeteria. Roger came by the table, but he was by himself. He sat down across from me, and he unpacked his lunch and started eating.

Can you believe that? He just started eating and didn't say anything, one way or another. But every couple of bites, he would look over at me, like he was expecting to hear something.

I wasn't sure what he wanted. I felt bad for making him cry, but I wasn't about to say sorry. Maybe that makes me a bad person, but I couldn't apologize to someone who had bullied me since first grade. So I didn't say anything either. We ate our whole lunch that way. It was the weirdest lunch I've ever had, and that includes the time I ate fried frog legs.

When he ate the last bite of his peach cobbler cup, Roger finally spoke. Just a few words. They sounded half like a question. He said, "Principal Miller's...my dad...?"

I realized what he wanted to know. "I didn't tell anybody about it," I replied. Any of the other kids, I meant.

Roger just nodded his head and blew a long breath through his lips. He picked up his tray to go. He turned back one last time and said, "My dad's not a bad guy. All right?"

Then he went off. And now I think we're okay. We're not friends or anything. He hasn't said a word to me since. But we're okay now.

I have to start my homework now. (I have to draw a boring diagram of a boring plant cell and label all of its parts for boring Mr. Cesar.)

Have a good weekend,

Felix

P.S. Even though Roger is leaving me alone now, I'm not going back to the cliffs near the hotel. I don't want to, and I don't need to. Not anymore. I found a better place. Quin showed it to me.

Attachment: Sept_23.jpg (276 kb)

Hi Marcus,

I was hoping Quin would call this weekend. You said that after the sixth week of Basic Training, soldiers are allowed phone privileges on the weekends. Well, it's been six weeks now, and no call from Quin.

We were all hoping to hear from him. I asked Mom if she ever worries about him, and she told me, "Every day and twice on Sundays." We had a good talk yesterday while I helped her at a photography gig. It was a big beach party for some rich girl's eighteenth birthday. I followed Mom around with her lens bag and backup memory cards for the camera. I've been helping her a lot lately. I started helping when I was suspended and couldn't watch TV at all.

Anyway, it's a big letdown and I'm feeling bummed out about it. The fog that's settling over Ocean View Avenue isn't helping, either. It makes our whole block look haunted.

I keep thinking that maybe Quin forgot about us. But that's silly. The drill sergeant at Fort Benning is probably just extra tough and won't give my brother a break.

Down in the dumps,

Felix

Dear Marcus,

I'm sorry you are not feeling well. It must be horrible to be cooped up at the hospital for such a long time. And because your library is closed on the weekends, you don't even have the Internet to connect you to the outside. I'll bet you feel like you're missing a lot. I know that would make me sad, too.

I'm not sure if this will help you feel better or not. I hope it does...you've never talked to me like you did in your last letter. I'm worried about you.

A couple of weeks back, when I was being all "dramatic," I told you that I opened Quin's envelope. But I never said what was inside, or what I did with it.

I'll back up to the beginning. This story starts on September the 6th, the day I punched Roger. You probably remember what I wrote that day. I felt so terrible. I'd never gotten in trouble at school before, and I'd never made someone cry before, and I'd never let my parents down like that before. And I felt like I couldn't talk to anybody about any of it.

Before bed, I had a good, long cry about everything. I was feeling very sorry for myself.

But then I remembered the envelope Quin gave me at his Oath ceremony. He said to open it on "the worst day of my life." I figured it was time.

Inside the envelope...I found a second, slightly smaller envelope. And inside that envelope...I found a third envelope that was a little smaller. That made me smile. Quin is such a big goof.

The third envelope had Quin's writing on the front: "In case of emergency." I opened it and there were two pieces of paper inside. One was a map that Quin had drawn. The other paper was a letter. I'll copy down what it said.

Felix:

Since you are reading this letter, I know you must be having an awful time. If I'm wrong, and you're just fine...close this letter back up and quit sneaking peeks, Peanut-head!

Jokes aside...I'm sorry you're upset. Lucky for you, though, I have just the thing to cheer you up. I'm not going to tell you what it is—just how to find it.

Think of this like a treasure hunt. If you follow my map and the directions on the side, it should be no problem. No Googling! You'll ruin the surprise, and I'll know. Trust me, I have my ways.

Your wise older brother,

Quin

I don't know about you, but that sure grabbed my imagination. I had to wait out the night. But first thing in the morning, once Dad had gone to work at the shop and Mom had started on her sculpting, I told Mom I was going for a bike ride. (That was the only fun thing I was allowed to do during my suspension, since it counts as exercise.)

I followed the map south. It wasn't very detailed. It was basically just a bunch of lines for a few important streets, with arrows pointing the way. Each arrow had a number that matched up with instructions on the side of the page.

3) Turn left at the gas station.

6) Cut through the parking lot. The fence in the back is torn.

After a long, hot ride south, Quin's directions led off the streets and into the hiking paths in the woods. It was a bit tougher to ride, but the paths were wide enough that it wasn't so bad.

Take a left at the fork.

Take the second right.

I hoped that I had gotten everything right. When I stopped and looked at my cell phone to check the time, I found that I had no reception. If I got lost, there was no way to call for help.

Finally, I made it down to Quin's last instruction. It said: "Follow the path and look for the yellow flag. When you reach it, turn right and cut through the brush 'til you hit sand."

I was ticked off then. I didn't realize that he was just leading me to the beach! I wondered, "Why couldn't I have just skipped all these dumb directions and rode in a straight line down the coast?"

But since I had come so far, I decided to follow the instruction just as Quin had written it. I walked down the path, eyes peeled for a yellow flag. After about ten minutes, I found it. Sticking up out of the ground was one of the neon flags for Dad's ATVs. The thin metal post was planted in the ground so that the flag was only a few inches off the ground. I reached the flag and gave it a slap with my hand. Then I turned off of the path.

I could see streaks of light and blue ocean through the gaps in the trees. I moved toward it slowly—I had to walk my bike because the ground was all brush. And I grumbled the whole way, muttering about what a waste of time this was. There was beach land everywhere. What made this part so special?

Finally, the trees opened up and I was back in the sunlight. I stepped out of the brush, I planted my feet grumpily in the sand, and I looked out with a smirk that I hoped said, "What <u>now</u>, Quin??"

But then the smirk became a smile. The smile became a big dopey grin. And from there I just had to let my jaw hang. Because not fifty feet away, I saw a horse galloping down the beach. The horse was tall and dark brown with white down near its hooves. A young woman with long braids rode upon it, shaking the reins and asking for more.

The horse and its rider were not alone. I saw three other people, each of them riding a horse along the beach: a teenage guy in a Hawaiian shirt and blue jeans, a heavyset man with a mustache, and a woman with a big floppy hat. They were all moving slower, just at a trot.

I forgot about the problems on my mind. I just sat and watched them all ride. The woman with the braids joined the others and trotted at their speed. Sometimes, she would give the other riders instructions or correct them. I realized she must be their guide or teacher.

After a while, the braided lady spotted me sitting there. She waved and I waved back. She trotted toward me, close enough that I could hear the horse's heavy breath. Close enough to touch its shadow on the sand. It looked like a giant with the sun behind it.

The lady stroked the horse's mane. "Want to say hi?" she asked me.

I just shook my head no.

"Maybe next time," she said. She rode back over to the group, and they went back up a path in the woods. I sat there a little while longer and thought of Quin. My brother made up that whole little adventure just for me. And he showed me real horses like he said he would. Quin really gets me. It's good to feel understood. That's what I'll tell him if he calls.

I hope I told that story as clear as it is in my brain. And I hope it helps you.

Sleep well,

Felix

Dear Marcus,

I'm glad you liked the story. I did some looking around online after I saw the horses. The horses come from this neat ranch in the dunes. (That's where Quin led me, in his extra-complicated way. It's an area a few miles south of here.) It is called the Telosa Family Ranch. It works kind of like Dad's ATV shop, only they rent horses!

That's right. Tourists can borrow a horse from them and go for a ride right on the beach. There are riding trails through the trees and brush, too. There was a picture of the lady with the braids on the website. Kim is her name, Kim Telosa. She and her siblings are riding guides. Their father owns the ranch. I wonder if my dad ever hoped that Quin and I would work at his shop like that.

I think it's awesome that this horse ranch is there just a few miles from my house. It's so expensive to rent a horse, though! I did the math: I start collecting allowance again on October 7th. I would have to save every penny I get until Valentine's Day just to pay for a one-hour ride.

But…that's really kind of a good thing. I love horses, and they're awesome to look at. But when I saw one up close, I was actually a little scared of it. I'm embarrassed to say so, but it's true. Horses are so much bigger than they look in movies. And they're <u>strong</u>. The muscles in their shoulders are bigger than my head!

I think that's why I didn't pet the horse that day, when that Kim lady rode over to me. I got worried that maybe the horse wouldn't like me, or it wouldn't listen to me. It could go wild and just run me right over!

Still, I really liked watching. I'm going to go back this weekend. Maybe I'll take your advice and just write Quin a letter, instead of waiting for him to call. Why on earth didn't I think of that before? I guess I just assumed he couldn't get mail since he couldn't use the phone. I should have asked you!

Thanks for the tip,

Felix

Dear Marcus,

It sounds like you're still feeling lonely at the hospital. I'll bet it can be tough watching all of the families come and visit while you are stuck by yourself. But you're wrong about one thing. You're definitely not alone, because you've got me. It's not much, I know. But this weekend, remember that I'm rooting for you when you start to get down, or if you feel that ache that's not in your scars but somewhere deeper inside. I wonder about how you're doing all the time. I'd be happy to make you an honorary Maldonado, if you want.

Your "brother,"

Felix

Marcus,

I thought I'd write you a little note before I head off to school. I hope your weekend was okay. I had a nice Saturday and a great Sunday night. That's because...Quin called!

It was right before dinnertime. Mom put the phone on speaker so that we could all hear him. Quin says Basic Training is all long days and hard work. The worst part is not the training, though. It's the bugs. Quin says there are mosquitoes in Georgia as big as his fist! But he is making great new friends, and he feels so honored to be serving his country.

Quin also thanked me for the letter I sent. (I mailed it the day after you gave me the idea. It arrived at Fort Benning yesterday morning.) Quin said I described the trip really well. He was glad that he could cheer me up.

But that was not the main reason he called. Quin mostly wanted to tell us about his Basic Training graduation. It is only three Fridays away, you know. We can't afford to fly out to see it, but we won't have to miss out on the big day. Quin said that the Army will be taping the whole ceremony, and they will put it online for people to watch over the web!

We can't play video with our dial-up connection. It's too slow. So do you know what my dad said when he heard about the webcast? He said, "I guess we'll have to get an upgrade by then!" It was strange because we are headed into the off-season soon, which means less tourists and less money. Dad never, ever wants to spend extra money near the off-season, unless it's for a birthday or Christmas or something. Mom is looking for a high-speed Internet provider that we can afford.

I have more to write, but I need to go and get the bus to school. I have to catch it one block away, because my street is too narrow for it to turn onto. I'll be sending you something this afternoon. But it's not an email, so don't expect it for a few days.

Rushing out the door,

Felix

Salty Air,
Without a Care

Dear Marcus,

I hope this gets to you in time for the weekend. This is a very special postcard. First, it's a picture of a horse from the riding ranch. Actually, it is a mare. Her name is Frenchy. That is Kim, the braided lady, on her back. Second, the card is special because I made it myself!

I borrowed Mom's camera and I found Kim riding with another group. I was nervous about introducing myself, but Kim was so nice! She smiled, posed, and then went on her way.

Mom helped me put the quote on the picture using her computer. I wrote "Salty Air, Without a Care" because that describes the dunes near the ranch and how I feel when I go there. Also, it has a rhyme, which I noticed a lot of postcards have. I printed the picture on Mom's cardstock, and here it is!

Maybe if you put this by your bed, you will feel better at night. The horse could chase your bad dreams away or something. Frenchy might be a girl, but she looks pretty tough.

I hope this helps,
Felix Maldonado

P.S. I made a second copy to keep by my bed, too.

1LT Marcus Greene

WRNMMC

8901 Rockville Pike

Bethesda, MD 20889-5600

Dear Marcus,

I read some news that got me upset today. The National Guard called up another unit from SLO. I read about it in an article online. It is not Quin's unit, thankfully, but it's got me nervous all over again.

The members of this unit were probably going about their lives, working during the week, training on the weekends at Camp SLO or Camp Roberts up north. And now, without any notice, they have to pack up and go fight in Afghanistan. It's just so…fast. It isn't fair to their moms, dads, or little brothers.

I've had a thought stuck in my brain. It was easy for me to look up which units are home and which ones have left. But once they get out to Afghanistan, it's like they've disappeared. I can't find news about what the Guard units from SLO are doing out there. I really hate that. I think I'd feel better if things weren't such a big mystery.

It's just like with your Army unit. When you were attacked, I could not find any news stories about it. Why didn't the blogs and the newspapers write about it? It's real news, and it is very important! They write about all kinds of other stupid stuff, like movie stars and which one is dating which. Why not stuff that really matters?

Confused,

Felix

Dear Marcus,

I'm glad you got my postcard! Like I wrote, I hope it keeps you company this weekend. I looked at my copy for a while last night before I went to bed.

Thanks for trying to answer my questions about the news. I know you can't give me any specific answers. It just seems unfair to me. Actually, it's worse than unfair. It is <u>unjust</u>. (That's a social studies vocab word, and it's the perfect one to use.)

You guys deserve more attention, especially the soldiers who are hurt. I guess there's not much I can do about it, though…aside from gripe to you all the time, ha-ha.

Your caring pal,

Felix

Dear Marcus,

I would have written on Monday, but the cable company was over installing our new Internet connection. That's right...we finally have broadband! It is so much faster. The pictures just load up like, "Pop! Here's your webpage!"

I did something I am very proud of this weekend. I was feeling really down because of all the stuff I wrote to you about, so I went back to the dunes to watch the horses and cheer up. But on this visit, I tried to be a little braver than before. When Kim rode over to say hello, I asked if I could pet her horse, Frenchy.

I was anxious at first, but Kim said you can't touch a horse nervously, because it can sense that and it will make the horse upset. "You have to use a firm hand," Kim told me. She showed me how to hold my palm out and let the horse sniff my hand. Once Frenchy knew my scent, I could pat her side.

I don't know how to describe what it felt like to actually touch a horse. I don't want to sound silly or wishy-washy. But I could feel her lungs working under my hand, and they were so steady and powerful. When I felt them, my brain just went calm. It was even better than when I used to sit at the cliffs.

That's all I've got for today. I just wanted you to know that I tried something new.

Talk to you soon,

Felix

Dear Marcus,

It's okay that you have not had much time to write this week. Your physical therapy work-out sounds tough, so it makes sense that you'd need to rest after.

I haven't had much time, either. It's been a really busy week with school and the big festival that happened in town over the weekend. It's called the Pismo Beach Clam Festival. It's the last big event of the year here before tourist season ends and off-season begins. It gets very crowded and Dad has a lot of customers.

Usually I want to see the parade we have in town (it's even bigger than the 4th of July one, believe it or not) but Dad needed my help since Quin isn't around. I didn't mind. I haven't been very big on clams lately, I guess. Dad let me run the register for a little while, and I hosed down the ATVs in the parking lot when they were returned.

So that was my weekend. Aside from that, I've been working on an assignment for science class. I had to make a shoebox diorama of an animal and its habitat. A whole lot of kids in my class are making little beaches with holes where clams live. Not me, though. I'll give you one guess which animal I picked.

You're pretty smart, so you probably guessed "horse." Which is right! I tried to make a model of the Telosa Family Ranch and their stables. I turned it in today. I worked extra hard on it, and Mom helped me, too. It turns out that she's pretty great at dioramas. I guess they're kind of like those sculptures she makes out of junk, but smaller.

I hope Mr. Cesar likes my work. I've decided that I want to be a veterinarian when I grow up, so I need to get all "A"s in science so I can get lots of scholarships. I don't know how far back colleges check for that kind of thing.

Busy like a bee,

Felix

Dear Marcus,

Today, Quin graduated from Basic Training! We just watched the video online. I won't go into too much detail since you were part of the same ceremony yourself last year, but it was so neat to watch everyone march in their uniforms. I'm not sure why, but I felt really different from when Quin first joined the Guard in August. I didn't even mind that Quin blended in with all the other graduates and we couldn't pick him out of the crowd.

Anyway, Quin's not all finished, as you know. He still has his advanced training to do. It starts next week in Virginia and will last until December. But now that he's finished Basic, I can say that my brother is a real soldier. I am so proud of him!

I wasn't the only proud Maldonado. I spied on my dad a bit while we all watched the video. He was smiling, and his eyes were all wet and glassy, just like when Quin finished high school.

Feeling pretty good,

Felix

P.S. I guess it's not too important compared to everything else, but I got the grade back on my diorama. That bum Mr. Cesar only gave me a "B+." We were supposed to show an animal in its "natural habitat," so he said that showing a horse in a stable was not quite right. I should have made grasslands or plains, or something like that. He said it showed "great effort." I guess that's something.

Dear Marcus,

First off, thanks for writing all those nice things about my brother. The next time I write to him, I'll definitely pass on your congratulations, and also your advice.

Speaking of writing letters, I got a big idea today. It came during language arts. You see, Mr. Dulac announced a new class project. Really, though, it's a project for everyone in second grade and up. We are all going to write letters to soldiers again.

It turns out that our principal liked Mrs. Seymour's letter project from last year so much that he is instructing everyone to do it this year. The only difference is that instead of writing for Memorial Day, we will be writing in honor of Veterans' Day.

I think it's nice that more kids will be writing letters to soldiers. But I think I have a more creative idea for how we can do the project. Tell me if you think this is any good.

Remember how I sent you the postcard I made a few weeks ago? Instead of writing to soldiers who are in battle, I'd like for everyone in my class to make cards for the hurt soldiers at your hospital. My mom could help make the postcards. Once they're made, the whole class could write to soldiers who don't have a lot of visitors. Maybe it would make them feel better. What do you think?

If you like the idea, I could use your help. You could tell me which soldiers are most badly hurt, or the ones who you think could use a pick-me-up. Each kid in my class could be matched to a specific one. It would be nicer to write a letter to an actual person, instead of that plain "Dear Soldier" thing we did last year.

Besides me, there are twenty-two kids in my class. Do you think you could find twenty-two soldiers for the others to write to? Please let me know what you think. I have to tell Mr. Dulac soon if I am going to ask him to change the project.

Thanks a million,

Felix

P.S. I almost forgot. I attached a picture of me with my diorama. Thanks for asking to see it!

Dear Marcus,

I'm really glad you liked my postcard idea. I went and had a talk about it with Mr. Dulac after school today. I was nervous about talking with him. He's a good teacher, but I've mostly kept to myself at school since my fight last month. I guess I got a little used to that. I was afraid that I'd tell Mr. Dulac my idea and he would say it was dumb or a waste of time.

But I stayed back after the last bell, and we talked. You know what? Mr. Dulac really liked the idea. He said it was very thoughtful and original. He was impressed that I have been writing letters to you for so long, and he was very interested in hearing about Quin and everything that's going on at home.

There is only one problem that Mr. Dulac brought up. He said if we are going to change this project like I want, we can't do it for only our class. We have to do it for the whole fifth grade so that his other classes don't raise a fuss. So I won't need twenty-two soldiers' names. I'll need sixty-eight.

I'm sorry to change the plan on you like that. Is that okay? You said there are thousands of soldiers at Walter Reed, so I hope it won't be too hard for you. You'd have about a week to get the names to me, so you don't have to rush all around the hospital grounds or anything. Maybe your friend Nurse Hunt could help gather names if it is more work than you want to do.

I'm so excited to start!

Felix

Dear Marcus,

Thanks so much for getting that list of names together. (Thank Nurse Hunt for her help, too.) All of the fifth grade kids are supposed to turn in the pictures they want to make into postcards tomorrow. Mom said they can give a CD with a picture or a drawing that she can scan into our computer and shrink down.

I'm really glad I've got this postcard project to keep me busy. This is kind of a weird time in Pismo Beach. For most places, October 31st just means "Halloween." Here, though, the end of October also marks the start of the off-season. I've brought it up before. In the off-season, Dad closes his shop an hour earlier each day, and he does not even open the shop on Sundays or Mondays. That is because the tourists don't come around as much in the fall or winter. The off-season is a real downer. Pismo Beach seems a lot bigger without all of the tourists.

Kind of like my room without Quin. It's been better since he and I started writing, but it's still not as good as looking across the room and saying, "Hey, you awake?"

Anyway, I've got to go have breakfast and get ready for school.

Thanks for being there,

Felix

DATE: Thu., Nov. 3 at 6:52 p.m.
SUBJECT: Postcards

Dear Marcus,

Boy, it takes a lot of time to make each of these postcards. Now I see why Mom makes one design and prints a lot of them to sell, instead of making unique, individual ones.

Except for a couple of kids who were late, Mr. Dulac collected everyone's artwork on the 1st. Mom and I have been turning it all into postcards since. I scan each picture using her little scanner, and Mom showed me how to shrink them to the right size and how to fix the colors so that they will print nicely when it's time. (I still need some help getting that part just right.)

I'm taking a break right now to say hi, but there are still a bunch of cards left to do before tomorrow. They have to be ready for school tomorrow so that everyone can write their messages on them over the weekend. Mr. Dulac needs to mail the postcards out on Monday so that they arrive in time for Veterans' Day.

So far, we've printed about fifty of the post-cards on Mom's heavy paper. Mom is cutting their edges with a paper cutter to make them all the perfect size. That means there are about eighteen cards left to prepare. It's going to be a <u>long</u> night.

Wish me luck,

Felix

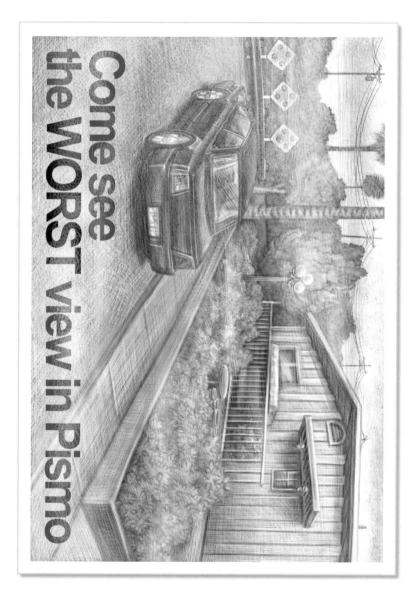

Hey Marcus,

Sometimes I don't know where my head goes. I was so busy making everyone else's postcards that I almost did not make one for you. But here it is. It's a picture of my house. In the fog. As always. (Ha-ha.) See what I mean about the view?

Everybody else will be turning in their postcards to mail today. They'll all say, "I hope your leg feels better," or "Please get well soon." But you already know I want you to get better. So here's what I'll say instead.

At some time in the next few months, you'll be cleared to leave the hospital. When you go, I hope you'll think of visiting my family in Pismo. We don't really have room for guests (unless you like sleeping in a bathtub)...but I hope you'll come by our town if you get time off from the Army. I talked to my parents about it. Consider yourself invited.

Happy Veterans' Day,

Felix Maldonado

Proud Owner, Worst View in Pismo Beach

1LT Marcus Greene

WRNMMC

8901 Rockville Pike

Bethesda, MD 20889-5600

165

DATE: Mon., Nov. 14 at 4:48 p.m.

SUBJECT: Happy Monday

Marcus!

It sounds like you guys had a really nice Veterans' Day. I'm so happy that the postcards all came in! Are some of the soldiers really going to write back? That's awesome news. I won't tell anybody, though. I'll let it be a surprise. It was such a cool surprise the first time you wrote to me. I don't know if you've been able to tell, but you've really made a difference in my life.

I have to get going now. Mom wants to take me out shopping. Since my birthday is coming up (on Sunday!), she wants to take me out so that I can help pick out a present. She said I can donate my old cell phone to the Red Cross and get a new one...one with a camera built in! That way, I can take pictures whenever I want. So expect a lot more attachments!

Your pal and soon-to-be-birthday-boy,

Felix

DATE: Fri., Nov. 18 at 6:11 p.m.

SUBJECT: Responses

Hello Marcus,

Some letters came for kids in my grade yesterday. They arrived at school and Mr. Dulac handed them out during language arts. Not everybody got a letter, but the ones who did were so happy! They were getting passed around during lunch like they were prizes that the kids had won.

Even Roger Batista was in a great mood. His soldier wrote back. Lupe and Kenneth did not get letters, so he bragged his head off all during lunch and recess. He looked over at me one time for just a second, and I could swear that he smiled at me.

All my happy classmates were fun to watch, but thinking back on it, I'm a little bummed out. That's because I was hoping I would hear from you, too. I had hoped I might have a birthday letter waiting in the mailbox when I got home today. Or an e-card that played "Happy Birthday" or something.

It's okay, though, I'm not mad or anything. I had just hoped to hear from you, that's all.

Have a nice weekend,

Felix

Dear Marcus,

So, I turned eleven today. It has been a pretty great birthday, even if I did not hear from you. I did hear from another soldier, at least, because Quin called me up!

I should really start from the beginning, though. I got two great presents on the morning of my birthday. The first was the camera phone I picked out with Mom earlier this week. It is a "refurbished" phone, which basically means "used but not abused." I might be abusing the phone, though. I've already taken almost a hundred pictures with it.

The other present was a fishing pole from Dad. He has Sundays off now since it's the off-season. As the second part of my present, he took me fishing today up at Dinosaur Caves Park!

Weirdly enough, Dinosaur Caves Park doesn't have any huge caves. And the closest things they have to dinosaurs are these dinky little carved statues of baby dinosaurs popping out of eggs. I guess there used to be caves and a really big dinosaur statue that stuck right out of the water, but the cave collapsed and the dino fell apart long before I was born.

Anyway, there are still some good fishing spots, so that's where we went. Dad and I had a great time even though we didn't catch much. We didn't talk too much, either. Dad's never been a very big talker. But I did get to ask about one thing that's bugged me. It was a question I've had banging around in my head since the summer.

I didn't dive right in. First, I started with a different question. "You think Quin will call tonight?" I asked. (I wasn't sure then.)

"I'll bet he will," Dad replied. "Kid's got a good head on his shoulders."

"You're pretty proud of him now, huh?"

Dad nodded. "He's really finding his own way. Though, you know, you're turning out pretty great yourself."

He squeezed the back of my neck through the floppy fishing hat I was wearing and gave me a little shake.

So then I asked my real question. "Dad, how come you never finished college?"

He rubbed that spot at the top of his forehead. Finally he said, "I guess I got scared."

"Scared of what?" I asked.

He laughed. "Scared of everything, Peanut."

I think I understand what he meant. But you know what? Dad is happy working at the ATV shop. I guess you don't have to be brave all the time, and things can still work out.

Anyway, once it cooled off, we packed up the two little runt fish we had caught and went back home.

Then, right between dinner and my birthday cassava cake, Quin called. He said this was not a speaker phone call. He wanted a heart-to-heart with his "little bro." (Meaning me!)

Quin is halfway through his advanced training, which means he'll be finished in four weeks. He'll be done just in time for Christmas! He got himself set up with a part time job repairing the National Guard trucks at Camp SLO. I felt so happy to hear the news that I could have passed out right then and there. If the Guard gave Quin a job there, I guess that means he really will be coming home!

He doesn't get much free time during this part of his training, but Quin is also trying to see if he can start at Cal Poly next semester. He might be able to just make the cutoff to apply, but he said if not, "There's always the fall." He was a lot more upbeat than I've heard him sound about college.

After Quin finished telling me about himself, he asked me about our postcard project. I mentioned it the last time I wrote to him. I told Quin all about it. When I got to the end of the story, he said something that I'll never forget.

Quin said, "You might be a little shrimp sometimes, but you've got a big enough heart for the both of us."

I don't know about all that stuff about having a big heart. I just thought those postcards would be a good thing to do. But I'm so glad I could make him proud. And I'm even gladder to learn he is really coming back home.

This was an almost perfect birthday. Almost perfect.

Happy birthday to me,

Felix

P.S. Here is a picture I took with my camera phone. It's Dinosaur Caves Park. On the left is my dad. On the <u>nowhere</u> is a whole bunch of dinosaurs. (Ha-ha.)

Dear Marcus,

Oh, wow! Wow! You didn't forget. That was so worth the wait. I can't believe you got all those soldiers together to sing me "Happy Birthday"! It was way better than a letter or an e-card.

You are the best friend I could ever ask for. I saved the video you sent the moment after I watched it. I wish I could show everybody what you did for me. I'll bring a copy of the video in to show Mr. Dulac, for sure. As long as he promises not to show it in class, that is. It would make my classmates green with envy! (I read that in a book last month.)

Thanks for sharing the good news about your arm, too! It's so nice that you will be discharged from the hospital next month. And you'll be out right about the same time that Quin comes home. How cool is that?

Quin flies back home on December 17th, the day after he finishes advanced training. When will you find out the exact day you can leave? Are you free to do what you want after? Or do you have to go back to your Army base and help out there?

Anyway, I don't want to bug you with questions. You might not even know what you're doing yet. But thanks so much again for the video. I'm going to watch it another time!

You are awesome,

Felix!

P.S. Hope you like that picture. That is my HAPPY FACE! (ha-ha)

P.P.S. In case I don't get a chance later this week, happy Thanksgiving!

Attachment: Nov_21.jpg (284 kb)

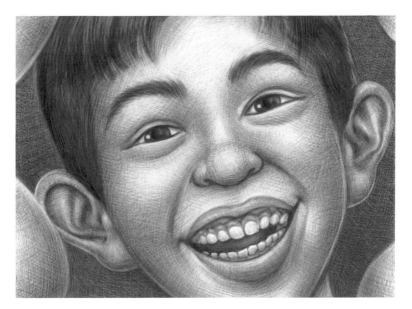

Dear Marcus,

Sorry I've been quiet so long...I've been cleaning, cleaning, cleaning. That's because the day after Thanksgiving, Mom took a good look at my room and said, "Where's your brother going to sleep when he gets back?" I guess I'd kind of stopped doing my weekly room cleaning and just started piling stuff on Quin's bed instead. And don't even ask about the stuff I crammed <u>under</u> the bed.

But never mind all that. I marked the date you said on our fridge calendar. December 21st—Marcus checks out! It's a pretty awesome coincidence. That's also the day I start my winter break from school.

I'm so happy for you, Marcus. In nineteen days, you'll be free from the hospital and on the road. It's nice that you get a whole three weeks of time to yourself before you have to report back to Fort Riley.

I like your idea of "wandering around." It sounds like the perfect thing to do after being stuck in one place for so long. Are you really just going to hop on a train and see where it leads? It can't be too much of a surprise...it's on a track, you know.

Just kidding. It sounds like a neat adventure. I'll bet you can see a lot of cool things from a train. There are tracks all over the place, so you can go pretty much anywhere. Remember that train track that I said runs near my house? It's actually part of a line that stretches all up the coast. A train runs on it every day from San Diego to San Luis Obispo. I don't know if you were aware.

I'm not sure how the train line here would connect to you out in Washington, DC. But I'll bet the view on our train is the best around. A much better "ocean view" than the one I've got on my street, ha-ha.

I'd love to talk more about trains, but I've still got a trainwreck of my own to finish cleaning! So I'd better go. Keep me posted on your plans. Will you have Internet on the train?

Straightening and dusting away,

Felix

Dear Marcus,

So, I think this is going to be my last email to you. Don't worry, I'm not mad. Why would I be? It's just that I want to save some stories for when you get out here!

Did you really mean it? Are you really going to come and visit once you get out of the hospital? I'm still just…wow. You might have to forward me a copy of your train schedule, just so I know you aren't yanking my chain.

Gosh. My brother will be home for Christmas, and my best friend will be here right after New Year's. I have the whole first week of January off from school, by the way. So we can hang out no matter what day you get in.

I don't know what fun stuff we'll do yet. It might be too cold to go clamming on the beach. It's getting into that see-your-breath time of year, and the high tide is icy cold on your ankles. But we could go to my dad's shop and take an ATV for a ride (if you drive and we wear hoodies to keep warm). Or if you're up for some exercise, we can get you a Rent-a-Bike and Quin and I can show you the prettiest spots in Pismo. But I guess all the details can wait.

All I know for sure is that whatever we do, I will take lots and lots of <u>pictures</u>.

Speaking of pictures...I expect to see some evidence from each of the stops you make on your train trip. I don't want anything expensive, like a refrigerator magnet. Maybe just a postcard. A postcard would be perfect.

Until I see you,

Felix Maldonado

All right, all right. I know I said I'd hold off on the emails until I met you in person. But once again, I just couldn't wait. I need to tell you about one last thing. Think of this email as a big long P.S.

Quin called the house tonight. He graduates in six days, you know, and he flies back home in a week. Usually he wants to have a talk with the whole family when he calls. But tonight he just called for me.

The first thing I told Quin about was how you're coming to see us in a few weeks. He is really excited to meet you! I made him promise to drive us into SLO so that we can all go see that hockey movie together.

"All right," he told me. "But there's something you're going to have to do for me. Call it a trade."

I had a thought of what he might ask. "I'm not going up to Shark Beach. No way, no sirree."

Quin laughed. "That's the brother I know and love," he said. "No, it's something else. When do you start your break?"

I told him the day.

"Clear your calendar," Quin told me, "because I'm taking you riding at Telosa Ranch."

My tongue felt all thick and I couldn't even say a full sentence. "I—I—"

"You—you—you've got nothing to say about it," Quin replied. "You and I are going for a ride and that's that. See you in a week, Peanut-head!"

And that was our call.

It was hard enough to work up the guts to even touch a horse. But to actually sit in the saddle? To trust that this giant beast will follow my lead, and listen to my voice, and not just dump me under its hooves? It's a scary thing to imagine.

But you know what? I'm not going to back out. I think I can ride. I might be crazy, but I think it'll be all right.

Acknowledgements

First, I have to thank Jane Price and Kellie Hamilton, and all the people who make the wheels turn at Midlandia Press. I also owe a lot to Amy Hercules and my colleagues on the Lincoln Interactive team. Without all of your support, this book would never have made it past the outline stage.

I would be remiss if I did not thank my wife, Jenn, whose eyes are always the first to fall upon anything I write, and who, while I am drafting a new project, puts up with my waking her up late at night to talk out my ideas.

Tremendous thanks must go to Staff Sergeant Thomas W. Tkocs, Army National Guard, who provided me invaluable insight into the workings of the ANG and helped to guide me toward the answers I needed.

Lastly (or, as Felix might put it, "P.S."), I'd like to acknowledge the important work being done by organizations such as the American Red Cross and Any Soldier® to connect everyday citizens with soldiers serving abroad. If you find yourself inspired to write to a serviceman, but do not know where to begin, either organization would be a great place to start.

About the Author

Michael Scotto has worked as a filmmaker, a saxophone player, and an engineer's assistant, but his true passion has always been writing. A graduate of Carnegie Mellon University, Mr. Scotto is the author of the Tales of Midlandia picture book series, as well as the middle-grade novel *Latasha and the Little Red Tornado*. He currently lives with his wife and their very naughty dog in Pittsburgh, PA. For his civic contributions to the region, he was honored in 2011 by *Pittsburgh Magazine* and PUMP as one of the "Pittsburgh 40 Under 40." *Postcards from Pismo* is his second novel.

Learn more about him at *www.michaelascotto.com.*

About the Illustrator

In addition to his work on *Postcards from Pismo*, Dion Williams is a contributing artist to the Tales of Midlandia picture book series. He has worked for high-profile clients such as Disney, Warner Bros., and Nike, providing sculpting and art direction. Dion's diverse background has enabled him to bring versatility and ingenuity to Midlandia Press. When not working, he enjoys bike riding, home improvement, and good movies.